KIRSTEN MBAWA

Sagas of Anya

Printed and bound in Great Britain by Cloc Book Print, 10, Millmead Business Centre Mill Mead Industrial Centre, Mill Mead Road, Tottenham, London N17 9QU.

First edition

ISBN: 978-1-916-22621-0

Editing by James Taylor-Loftus

Proofreading by James Taylor-Loftus

Cover art by Goran J Tomic

Illustration by Olena Vecchia Pittura

Dedication
For my entire wider family who have been extremely supportive along the way and for my little sisters, Aiyven and Kaitlyn, whom I love so very much.

Acknowledgements

Without the grace and gift of God, this book would never have happened. So, first and foremost, thanks and glory go to God for all His blessings.

I am extremely grateful to my mum and dad. The road to publishing has been very fulfilling but sometimes hard. I'll admit there were times I wanted to give up, but my parents encouraged me to push through the writing blocks and challenges to eventually publish Sagas of Anya. They helped us every step of the way with things like finding the perfect people to work on the project, proof-reading, printing sample copies and so much more. It also must be extremely difficult to be running a publishing project for *two* books at the same time so thank you for bearing the weight of it!

I am also very thankful to my sisters, Aiyven and Kaitlyn, who have been very supportive and for letting me write in peace...mostly! Special thanks go to Aiyven, who has also written a book of her own — *"Land of the Nurogons"*.

She gave me some very good feedback too as well as constructive criticism to help my book be the best it can be.

Our family — grandparents, aunties, uncles, cousins, and close family friends have been very supportive and encouraging throughout — not just in words but also through the backing of our Kickstarter campaign. I want to say a big thank you to all of you. It's a blessing and it feels very reassuring to know we have your support at all times. May God bless you all.

Our Nanny, Nana JuJu, has been *so* understanding and supportive throughout our writing journey. In fact, her idea to enter the BBC 500-word competition is what started it all. Thank you so much, Nana Juju, we love you!

To all my school friends who shared the joy, called me "famous" and asked for my autograph! Thank you for your uplifting praise and for giving me one way to build my self-esteem! I cannot forget my school and teachers, Mrs Chapman, Mrs Peto, and many more who have celebrated this achievement and helped us get more awareness for our Kickstarter campaign by featuring us in the school newsletter. You have been very encouraging throughout this process. Thank you so much for boosting my confidence.

A big shout out also goes to the Chronicle and Echo newspaper for featuring us and to Alastair Ulke for carrying out our first-ever newspaper interview.

We appreciate your contribution to the achievement of our Kickstarter funding goal.

To everyone who backed, supported and shared our Kickstarter campaign, we would like to express immense gratitude. Putting your faith, goodwill and money into our project meant the world to us and we hope your encouragement fuels us to keep on writing.

Finally, but never the least, this book would not be what it is now without the following brilliant people, so one last, massive thank you to James the editor, Olena the Illustrator and Goran the cover designer. James, although tough at times, has helped so much with the proof-reading/editing and other general but extremely useful publishing advice. Working with James opened my eyes to so many new things about the publishing process. Olena has been very patient with my view of what the characters should look like and her drawings always succeed in astounding me! Finally, Goran, who has created some AMAZING cover designs, animations and more. Thank you all.

Anya

Mrs Axton

Tippets House

Mam

Tad

Contents

One

When Life was Saga Free

~~~

*M*am and I headed for the arcade leading off Splott Market. Women selling fancy silks walked briskly by and men with mugs of ale lined the walkways. One would have thought they would know better than to spend their waking hours steeping themselves in their brew. The arcade had the waft of fresh food about it but there was also that rank smell of drink hanging in the air. I could barely hear myself think with all the chatter, laughter and shopkeepers haggling for customers. We turned the corner towards the Cardiff docks. The cold, fresh air rouged our cheeks and our hair flew in the wintry wind as we walked down the cobbled street. The docks were rather drab what with the old, tattered shops.

Mam needed eggs and milk so we walked into one of the little corner shops lining the docks.

There were shelves of fruit, dairy products and vegetables. At the opposite end of the shop, a middle-aged man sat sprawled on a brown, leather chair.

He had light-brown hair so scraggly I could have mistaken it for straws. The man held a cup of ale in one hand and a sack of money in the other. Standing safely behind Mam, I watched as she studied the man. The cashier looked terrified. She was a small woman, probably my height with long, blonde hair and turquoise eyes.

The man grunted, stood up and staggered towards us. Now, I had a chance to take a proper look at him and my goodness, he was stocky! His arms were the size of logs. Big logs. His legs were so chunky a cow couldn't have produced more meat.

"Good day, sir," Mam said calmly, "Please excuse us, we need to buy some groceries."

She tried to step around him but he quickly blocked her path.

"I'm the boss," stated the man. His voice sounded like nails scratching down a chalkboard.

"That's lovely but I need to get through," she stated firmly, making the mistake of trying to push him out the way, "and, I don't really like your drink-filled breath in my face thank you very much."

2

The man's face turned red and he lifted his fist but just in time I grabbed her hand and pulled her outside.

"Oi!" the man shouted, running towards us.

"Get back 'ere!"

"Anya, run!" Mam commanded as if that wasn't my first instinct.

We ran like our lives depended on it, which they in fact did — turned corners, ducked into alleyways, and hid behind stalls but the man kept close on our tail.

The other end of the docks were in sight. I could see the water gleaming in the sun.

Soon, I realised we were heading straight for the water but we kept going. I stopped at the very edge but Mam didn't.

"Mam, watch out!"

It was too late. She plunged into the water and I watched in horror as her body sank down into the murky depths.

* * *

I woke up, gasping for air.

I touched my face. It was wet. I wasn't sure if it was sweat or tears. I ran into Mam and Tad's room, sobbing.

"Anya, dear, whatever is the matter with you," asked Tad sitting up.

"The gangster Tad, I had a nightmare and he was…"

Tad held me close as I narrated the events of my nightmare.

"You know that night I saw that horrible man; it was very late, Anya. Nothing like that can or will ever happen to you."

"B — but you said he was evil and a brute and violent and…"

"Don't get yourself into a state, Anya. It was just a silly dream. That's all."

I hugged Tad for a few minutes before returning to my room and slipping back into my bed.

Tad had told me stories about the notorious gangster who roamed the streets of Cardiff in the dead of night.

"It was as dark as Egypt," Tad would start, "and I was hurrying back home. The wind was tugging at me but I ploughed through it. I heard footsteps coming from the alleyway and started to increase my pace. The footsteps grew louder and faster and when I turned around — there he was! The brute, the demon. It was none other than Bron Lewis. He stared at me with coal-black, empty eyes. He was dressed entirely in black and I would not have been able to see him if were not for his uncovered nose and eyes. My mind was telling me to run away as

5

fast as I could but my legs kept me frozen to the spot. I practically saw my life flash before my eyes." Tad stopped.

"Oh, Tad! Do carry on." I pleaded.

"I am afraid it is your bedtime, my love," he replied.

"Please!" I opened my eyes wide and pouted.

"Oh, alright then. So, where was I? Oh yes.

The poor specimen of a man advanced towards me. He clicked his knuckles as he got closer and closer. Oomph! The man was knocked off his feet by none other than the police. I felt an urge to hug the officers but I simply thanked them and returned home. They arrested Bron Lewis for theft, arson and suspected murder. Rumour has it he'd escaped from prison but nobody has seen him since…"

* * *

Well, I must introduce myself. I'm Anya Rees. I am eleven years old, an only child and my parents love me dearly. I am known to be given to nightmares. Vivid ones. We live on Coveny Street and I attend Moorland Primary school, about a mile's walk away. Thank God Tad could afford the school fees; Moorland was not the grandest of schools but it was certainly a far cry from the dreaded Ragged Schools attended by orphans from the cholera infested housing courts of Womanby Street.

This morning was unusually sunny for early spring. I washed, scrubbed and brushed out my dishevelled, brown hair. I heard my mam, Maria, singing downstairs. Relieved she wasn't really falling off the edge of the docks, I skipped down to meet her. I was greeted with the scrumptious smell of buttered toast and sizzling bacon.

"Smells delicious!" I exclaimed, sitting down at the table.

"You think so?" She came around to me and placed two rashers of bacon on my plate, a slice of toast and a kiss on my forehead.

Mam is absolutely beautiful. She has dark-brown hair she never ties up, her smile shines like shimmering stars and her eyes have a perpetual sparkle in them. Charmingly pretty as she was, the doctors had told her her heart was weak and she suffered from epilepsy which gave her occasional fits.

I tucked in rapidly, relishing the delicious taste of Monday breakfast whilst Mam busied herself with the rest of the breakfast. I stuffed the last of the bacon into my mouth, hoping to banish the fright my nightmare had caused me.

I was just about finished, when my tad, William, came downstairs, a copy of the Cardiff Gazette tucked under his armpit. He looked rather suave in

7

his work clothes: a morning coat, stiff white collared shirt and a top hat. He worked as a clerk in the Cardiff Docks, built not too long ago by the Marquess of Bute. He wore fine clothes to work and often bragged that were it not for his grand job, we would be considered 'working class.' Not that being a middle-class clerk earned him any more than a fishmonger in Trinity Street's Central Market, Mam would sometimes quip when she was cross.

"You do look most handsome, Tad." I complimented him as he sat at the table.

"Thank you, my dear," he offered as he snatched the last bit of toast from my plate.

"Hey!" I declared, slapping his arm softly.
Tad chuckled and stood up from the table.
"I had better be going — I am already late as it is. I think I might have overslept."
She kissed him and I covered my eyes. I never wanted to get married.

"See you later my sweet." She called to Tad as he walked through the door.

"Off we go! Get your coat and satchel."
We set off, arm in arm, walking briskly and sharing funny memories of Tad's quirks and antics as we took the shortcut at the bottom of Marion Street.

"'Ello, lovelies," greeted Old Mo with her crookedly loving smile.

"Hello, Old Mo," I said.

"My you do look well today, Moa," Mam complimented Old Mo using her full name.

"Oh, come off it, Maria. You know I 'ate my full name. 'Moa,' 'Moa,' 'Moa.' The more I say it, the worse it gets!"

Mam laughed. "Where's Pat?"

"Gone off on one of her 'adventures' for some yarn I 'spose. Not sure how far she'll get since she's blind as a bat and as dumb as a dodo. She has a roaring fire in her stomach; I'll give her that."

"What are you knitting, Mo?" I asked." Just a shawl for a lady over on Constellation Street. She was all prim and proper too. 'La-dee-da, la-dee-dee.' I was shocked she wanted someone as filthy-looking as me to sew 'er a shawl, though I will modestly admit I am the best of the best," Mo boasted.

"Oh, Mo!" I giggled, "You do make me laugh."
As cheery as she was, Mo had not been so lucky with her children. She was Irish with a sea-faring husband who rarely came home. I remember when she had her tiny twin babies. Rumour has it Mo was so poor, they had died from the cold, harsh winter. Her eldest son, Thomas, fell in with the wrong crowd and before he knew it, was in Usk Jail. The next eldest was Gwenllian. She was a year older than me. She'd been sent to the workhouses last year when Mo struggled to feed even that one extra mouth. Mo missed Gwenllian dreadfully — you could tell by her gloomy face and glassy eyes. So she

took up knitting as an escape and, over the years, had gotten rather good at it. Pat was also in the knitting business which is how they had met. They had been inseparable ever since. Pat's birthplace was Cardiff, unlike Irish Mo, and was very old; although she was mad enough to claim to be in her twenties.

* * *

At the school gates, the other women stared and tutted at Mam saying, "look at her, she's as flat-chested as a slice of bread!" And "she's hardly got any bosom on her."

I think she noticed, but she chose not to make anything of it. She kissed my forehead a second time.

"Have a good day, my angel."

"Have a good day at work," I replied.

She kept a part-time job at a small cottage, where she would sew dresses whilst I was at school. Our school building was ancient with crumbling bricks, leaking roofs and floorboards with holes in them. There was a chalked out hopscotch and snakes and ladders area in the playground and benches for the older pupils to sit on and chat.

My best friends Annis and Sioned crept up on me, making me jump and yelp. I felt embarrassed.

"Guess what?" Annis enthused.

"What?" I questioned.

"We went to Mircove Beach together!" They said in unison. I must admit, I felt a bit envious they had gone to Mircove Beach without *me,* but I pretended to be pleased for them.

"That's nice to hear," I muttered glumly wondering to myself why they had not waited until the school holidays which would soon be upon us.

"Look, we're sorry we planned it without you but truly, you're always so serious about everything," Annis exclaimed.

"Hmm," Sioned agreed, looking embarrassed but agreeing all the same.

"Look, we have hoops."

"Good Ol' hoops." I lied, my eyes stinging from the tears welling up in them.

After what felt like decades of silence and nervous glances between Annis and Sioned, I offered a way out.

"Well, we had better get to class," and I ran into the school.

The whole school met in the main hall to pray. The first lesson was a girl's only lesson: Sewing. I wasn't sure which was worse, the teacher or the lesson itself.

Miss Evans taught it and she was absolutely horrid. Once, I had packed a small bag of Clove Rocks to share with Annis and Sioned. We ate some

11

during a break but decided to eat the rest if we got bored during afternoon lessons. Of course, we had to have sewing.

Annis 'psssed' to get my attention. She pointed to her mouth and then at me.

Checking Miss Evans wasn't watching, I reached slowly into my pocket and took out my bag of Clove Rocks. Turning around, I reached out my hand to Annis when...

"Anya Rees," Her aggravatingly level voice called Quick as a flash, I whipped my head around and stuffed my Clove Rocks back into my pocket.

"What do we have here?" Miss Evans asked as she walked over to me at a slow pace.

"Nothing, Miss Evans," I lied.

"It did not look like nothing to me, Anya Rees."

She wore a sinister smile as she yanked the bag of Clove Rocks from my pocket.

"What is this, Anya? Sweets? In my classroom?"

"No, Miss Evans," I stated untruthfully. "It is, in fact, my pills. Yes, I um, I have to take them in the morning, afternoon and at night. Yes, that's right. A — and my mam says if I don't take them, I will be as sick as a dog."

"Is that so?" Miss Evans mused.

"I shall not lie if I want to go to heaven," I asserted, even though I was not religious.

"I see. So, may I ask why you were passing your 'pills' to Annis?" Miss Evans was standing directly over me and I could feel her disgustingly warm breath on my neck.

"Well, uh." I scratched my head, "You see, Annis wanted some too because she is sick — isn't that so, Annis?"

Everyone turned around to look at Annis who went a rather dark shade of crimson.

"No."

I stared in complete shock at Annis. I felt betrayed.

Miss Evans turned to face me.

"So let us see what is really inside this bag shall we?"

That spiteful woman tipped my whole bag of Clove Rocks onto the floor. I had saved up for so long to buy them and now nearly half of them were gone.

"Come up to the front, Anya."

Oh, I had never been punished physically in school before and I was afraid today was that day. Unfortunately, I was right.

She took out a wooden ruler from her drawer, yanked my hands towards her and whacked the ruler onto my knuckles ten times. I tried my hardest to not show any sign of pain so she would not have the pleasure but I could almost see the happiness in her face as I whimpered.

Writing and Dictation lessons followed, which were much easier to bear. Eventually, it was time for a snack break; however, it was not long before we had to endure some more of Miss Evans. I kept pricking my fingers with the needles and ended up with blood-soaked cross-stitch — not that my work was any good in the first place.

Lunchtime finally arrived. Mam was waiting at the gates as normal to take me home for my customary slice of bread and cheese, washed down with a glass of water. Reluctantly, I walked back to school. *Time for more lessons,* I thought.

Back at school, I felt like horse manure. The morning hadn't gone well, I was bored stiff in Arithmetic and got severely told off for not concentrating, which was not entirely wrong as I ended up failing the test miserably. Reading and Geography were the only saving grace of the afternoon. By the end of the day, I was exhausted.

"Why so glum, treasure?" She asked stroking my face as she met at the school gates.

"Annis and Sioned went to Mircove Beach — without me!" I complained.

"Is that all?" she asked, laughing.

I glared at her. "It is not funny. I feel so left out."

14

"Listen, dear. You will always have some good friends and some who are less so. Maybe it's time you made some new ones?"

"No!" I exclaimed.

She sighed and looked at me. "Well, it's your choice, sweet. Come on, let's go."

A rather smelly homeless man sat on a battered-looking blanket begging passers-by for money with not much luck. He had a grimy face with pleading eyes. His hair was a damp mess and his clothes were tattered rags. I noticed he had cuts and bruises everywhere. Feeling sorry for him, we walked over. He looked up at us hopefully.

"Hello, sir," Mam said.

"Hello. Any spare change?"

She dug her hand into her small purse bag, on which I had somehow managed to embroider her initials and pulled out a farthing.

"I am dreadfully sorry, but all I have is a farthing," she stated apologetically.

"Oh, please don't be sorry. You're the only ones who have stopped by all day."

We bid him good-bye and walked on as birds chirped happily in nearby trees as the sky began to dim.

"What a lovely day." I agreed.

Children laughed with glee as they played in the park next to the school. We walked in silence until we arrived home.

* * *

As we got in, Mam said, "I'm not feeling that well..." Her skin was getting paler and paler as we entered the kitchen. She started clawing at her chest and turned around so her back was to me. She shook violently as she wheezed and coughed. I thought she was having a fit so I ran frantically to the medicine drawer in the parlour. While wondering if I was overreacting a little I fumbled through the drawer for her pills and dashed back.

Sitting down, she looked flushed. "What is all this fuss about Anya?" she asked a little breathlessly.

"It's your medication" I replied anxiously.

"You were coughing and wheezing and I thought you were having a fit so I..."

"Enough of this nonsense, Anya," she interrupted, "I am quite alright, dear. I'll just lay down for a while." I was unsure, but knowing she loved to be independent, I let her go upstairs.

I made her a ham sandwich with a mug of tea for when she got up and then sat in the living room to read, selecting one of Tad's books to pass the time. It certainly felt like I could do without making the effort to fetch one of my own from upstairs. It started to get cold. I put some kindling and logs into the fireplace and made a perfectly cosy fire.

It was getting chilly on the sofa so I laid by the fireplace and read. I got so absorbed in my book I was unaware at first how hot I was getting, so inched a bit further away from the flames. Mam came down after a couple of hours to make supper. She called me to come and help her cook it.

"Are you feeling better Mam? If you're not I made you a nice ham sandwich and a hot cup of tea, although it must be rather cold by now." I realised I was prattling a little.

"I'm fine now, Anya. Thank you though. Now you can help me prepare supper — you never know, you might need to cook for your own family one day."

"Never!" I exclaimed, secretly promising myself never to get married.

I chopped up some carrots and broccoli then dropped them into a pot of boiling water. Then I helped season and spice some pork, fetched some potatoes from the larder, sliced them up and placed them into the oven to cook.

Eventually, enticing smells started to emerge from the mouth-wateringly delicious food in the oven. Tad arrived soon after we'd set the table and I hugged him ferociously.

"Hello, Tad!" I cried.

"Hello, my dear. I do say, what has come over you? You're practically wrestling me. Look, I've something for you."

"Oh goody, I love presents." He handed me a long, thin package, which I snatched off him eagerly.

"Chocolate!" I exclaimed, breathlessly ripping off the wrap‑per.

"I don't think so," Mam interjected, snatching the chocolate from my hands. "You are about to have your dinner."

"Fine," I grumbled.

Tad chuckled and Mam took his jacket off to hang it up. "Yum. Smells amazing, Maria," Tad exclaimed, his eyes fixed on the pork.

"Thank you, darling, but I must say, Anya did a great deal of helping too."   To which I smiled.

"Two little cooks right here!" he cried.

We tucked into supper, me grabbing about four roast potatoes and Tad had over six!

Mam lectured us as she ate her second potato and chopped some pork up for me.

"I am not a baby, Mam; I can cut my own pork," I declared. I gobbled up noisily, smacking my lips as I savoured the last of the pork.

"Anya! I raised you better than to chew with your mouth open," she scolded.

"Sorry."

I sat awkwardly, jabbing my food with my fork.

"And for heaven's sake stop playing with your food, Anya Rees! If you do not want it, wash your plate and up to bed with you."

I washed my plate, bid them goodnight and went up to my bedroom. Reading my big book of fairy-tale kept me in good spirits before going to sleep. The next few days went surprisingly quickly, but that doesn't mean they were easy. I was over the moon when Saturday morning came. Finally. It was the school holidays and the beginning of one whole week without Miss Evans.

Breaking the silence over breakfast, Tad said, "Well, as you're not telling her, Maria, I will."

"What?" I questioned, inquisitively.

He inhaled. "We are going to…"

"We are going to Mircove Beach for the holidays!" Mam exclaimed. I stared at them in shock as Tad glowered at Mam.

"That was my line." He pouted.

I couldn't believe it. Mircove Beach! Then I remembered how Tad and Mam used to tease me mercilessly when I was younger.

Once Tad stuffed toilet paper in my shoes to fool me into thinking I had grown overnight. Another time he pretended to eat a fly he'd swatted when all the while, it was a raisin. Or when I sat down at the kitchen table and there was a wet, slimy frog there. Yuck!

"Sorry, but I'm not going to believe you just like that. The tricks you've played on me before are exactly like this."

"But it's true!"

"No."

"Yes," she insisted.

"Do not fib to me, Mam."

"Then where are all your clothes?" Tad asked.

"Probably outside drying" I quipped.

"The food?"

"Stored away."

"And my birthday?"

"Anya! You'll be in Mircove for your birthday. Come on, would we lie to you?" she asked.

"Yes, you would."

"A fair point."

We were suddenly interrupted by a double knock on the front door.

Mam got up but Tad said, "No, I'll get it."

She sat back down as Tad walked down the hallway to the front door. After a couple of minutes, he returned beaming from ear to ear.

"What?" we chorused.

"Fetch your bags, ladies, because we're off to Mircove Beach!"

Two

Traeth - Mircove Beach

T**ad** carried my brown, leather case down the stairs as I flapped about like a headless chicken, trying to get my books and art supplies together Mam had forgotten to pack.

"Mam! How could you forget my books and art things! I cannot go for so many days without them!"

"Sorry, my darling!" she replied.

Tad was leaning against the front door, patiently reading the paper.

21

"Are we ready?" he called.

"Not quite!" I called back.

"Well get a move on! The man will be trotting off with the carriage soon!"

I quickened my pace, now looking for a bag in which to put all my extra things. My bag search was unsuccessful so I had to carry my books and art materials with a great deal of beach discomfort. I whined and complained but Tad was not having any of it, insisting I was old enough to carry my things unaided.

Pulling the carriage was the most beautiful horse I had ever seen. It was a mare. Its silky brown coat gleamed in the sunlight. Around its hooves, nose and across its body were white spots. The horse whinnied and fidgeted, bored of standing still for so long. I eventually managed to stop gawping at the magnificent creature and we all bundled into the carriage.

"Never seen a horse before, missy?" the carriage driver enquired, laughing. "Where to then, my fine fellows?"

"Mircove Beach please" Tad responded.

After a while, I began to feel quite sick from the motion of the carriage. It didn't help that the carriage man wouldn't stop talking. Tad was merrily making conversation too. I wasn't sure if he was doing it for the sake of being polite or for the enjoyment of it. I wondered aloud why Tad had not arranged for us to take the train. I had never been on a train before and found the idea rather exciting.

"Because, my dear, it's very expensive."

"Oh," I replied, a little disappointed. Almost immediately I had another question ready. "How much longer until we get to Mircove Beach?"

"About another hour or so," Tad replied, shaking his head, but smiling.

I sighed and looked across at Mam. She was gazing contentedly out of the carriage window.

I must have fallen asleep because after what seemed to have been only a couple of minutes, we were there — Mircove Beach lay before us.

"We're here, we're here!" I gushed.

"Yes, we are!" said Mam rubbing her eyes. She had obviously been sleeping too.

Tad and the carriage driver unloaded the cases and passed them to Mam and me to arrange in a neat pile.

Mam gave the carriage driver tuppence for helping us and he tipped his hat at her as a sign of courtesy. As the man drove the carriage away, we turned to admire the stunning beach. It certainly lived up to my expectations. The sand was a brilliant gold and the sea — oh the sea! It was an intense turquoise and the waves splashed against the cliffs to the right at the other end of the beach as the water ebbed out and returned rhythmically. The water shimmered and sparkled as the shining sun reflected on its surface. There was a sign with an arrow. It read 'Traeth.' Like we needed to be told where the beach was. It was in full view.

"Blimey" I managed to say.

To the left of the beach were neatly arranged huts in all sorts of colours — red, orange, yellow, blue and green. On from the huts, and set back a little, was a bed and breakfast.

I was eager to run onto the beach, so I took the boots off my sweaty feet and charged towards the sea. Looking back, I saw Tad had also removed his shoes and was following the trail I had left in the sand to catch up with me. We were soon immersed in a game of hurling sand at one another. It was such fun we both got a little over-excited — I got sand in my mouth and Tad got some up his nose! At this point, Mam must have decided it best if we settled into the B&B as she called to where we were. We all walked excitedly to the B&B and knocked on the door.

* * *

A kind-looking woman greeted us, beaming broadly. "Well I'll be a monkey's uncle!" she exclaimed. "We haven't had a family of three for a very long time — do come in!"

The woman had brown hair tied up into a high bun, which was kept in place with a bow. She was both tall and broad and was wearing a fuchsia shirt with a long, spotted skirt which reached her ankles and brown booted feet. A white apron was tied neatly around her waist.

"I'm Betsy and I work here at Mircove B&B — of course!" Betsy insisted on giving us a tour around the bed and breakfast. "Follow me. This way please!" she beckoned invitingly.

First, we went to the dining area where we would have all our meals. Then the library in which I wanted to stay forever. Last on the tour were the bedrooms. Depending on how much you paid, you could have a small one or a large one.

"I'll show you the large bedrooms as you're a family — right this way" Betsy said.

The room was gorgeous! There was a double bed and a single bed. Each bed cover was decorated with a quilt of pretty and colourful flowers and birds. There was a window with a seat next to it — perfect for painting — and a large bathroom.

"Oh, please can we stay!" I begged them.

They chuckled in amusement. "It is beautiful but we have already paid for a smaller room."

The room my parents had paid for was tiny! It had no bathroom. Instead of a nice, clean toilet, there was a rough black chamber pot to one side which I found disgusting to look at and a clothing rack on which we would hang our summer clothes. The walls were mustard — dark mustard — and the floor was rough, almost coarse like sand but strangely, it did not stick to our feet which perplexed me for several minutes. I must admit, the small size of the room made it cosy and I laid my case down to unpack. Looking around the room, I spied a double bed to one side and just enough room for an armchair on the other. I was glad we had a double bed so I would be able to cuddle up with Tad & Mam; I know a big girl of eleven should not be cuddling up with her parents, but...

"Excuse me, but I must get downstairs to help prepare dinner in the dining hall. See you at dinner or breakfast maybe."

After we had packed away our things, we decided we ought to check out the attractions, so I changed into my sandals and a loose purple dress.

* * *

We had decided to return to the beach at first, but as soon as we had left the B&B I cried out "fish and chips!" and dashed for the beach hut as they chased after me. They eventually gave in to buying fish and chips and we all sat on the sand, tucking into our food.

"Thank you!" I mumbled stuffing my mouth with a handful of chips.

"You're most welcome," Tad answered, cramming some fish into his mouth.

Having wolfed down my fish and chips, I decided to fetch my art easel, canvas and painting supplies from the B&B so I could paint on the beach. Armed with my art supplies, we headed for a less crowded part of the beach. An old man was also painting. He was very good. His soft and gentle strokes across the canvas blended the colours together with wonderful effect. I wondered if I could get some tips from him but Mam & Tad didn't want me out of their sight.

I painted children and their families playing on the beach and people my age splashing in the water as if they were three. It was a greater challenge to paint the women and children who were in bathing huts on wheels being drawn into the sea by horses; that would have to be for another time, I thought. I must admit what I painted was not my best piece of work — I guess my heart was not really in it. Soon enough, I had my fill of painting so I asked Mam if I could paddle about in the sea. The tide had now gone out some distance so there was no need for a horse-drawn bathing hut.

"Please!" I begged.

"Alright, but be careful and stay where I can see you!" she called, but I was already running at full speed towards the water. I splashed about and dived into the salty water. Why did I open my eyes! They stung so badly! I tried to blink the salt out but it stayed in my eyes and kept stinging. I ran to mam who was reading serenely.

"Mam!" I cried.

"What's the matter, darling?" She asked sitting up, her voice full of worry. With my eyes watery and stinging, I couldn't see her face.

"My eyes! They sting!"

She rushed me to a public toilet where I could rinse out my eyes with fresh water, providing much-needed relief, though I decided *not* to return to the sea.

Afterwards, Tad suggested we might go for a walk along the pier. It wasn't long before what Mam and I thought was a wonderful idea started to frighten me. The pier stood high above the surface of the sea and I was a little terrified as we walked.

"This board looks looser than baby's teeth," I exclaimed, jumping two boards at a time.

"I promise you, it's sturdy, Anya," Tad implored laughing, "Look." He jumped up and down on the wood boards.

"Be careful Tad!" I warned.

The sky was cloudy but I could just see a few rays of sunlight peeking through. Many others were walking up and down the pier, but none looked as scared as me.

"Your teeth are practically clattering together!" Mam teased.

"Ha, haha," I murmured.

I begged to go and listen to the brass band on the beach and surprisingly they agreed even though it was getting late. Back onto the sweet, flat ground, we asked for directions to where the band was playing. Conveniently, the small bandstand was a short distance from the B&B, which meant we would only have a short walk back to our room.

Wooden deckchairs were arranged in curved lines in front of bandstand; on a raised platform under the roofed bandstand were four men. Most of their instruments were unrecognisable to me but I could just make out what looked like a large brass tuba. They played tremendously well, much to Mam's particular enjoyment. The band finished playing as the light began to fade, and upon returning to the B&B I collapsed onto my bed exhausted!

* * *

After breakfast the next morning, we headed out for another lazy day on the beach. I had forgotten my book in our room and returned to fetch it. On my way back to the B&B a boy about my age with curly ginger hair and a girl, about ten, with curly blonde hair approached me. I knew them both a little already, as we had exchanged glances and shy smiles the day before while listening to the brass band.

"Hello," they both said in unison.

"Hello," I replied.

"I'm Daisy and this is my older brother Frank."

"Nice to meet you. I'm Anya," I replied.

"Want to see something amazing!" Frank asked.

"Erm — well my parents...' I thought about how angry they would be if I left to go off somewhere without seeking their permission.

"You have to ask your parents if you can go places!" Daisy laughed.

"Well — yes but..."

"Baby" Frank stated derisively.

"I am not! Fine, I'll come. I'm sure they won't mind..." At least I *hoped* my parents would not mind.

"Wonderful" Daisy exclaimed, clasping her hands together. "Follow us."

Daisy and Frank led me behind the multicoloured huts and further down the beach. As we walked further and further away from my parents I felt increasingly worried about them. What would they think? Well, I wasn't going to let anyone tell me I was a baby so I kept on walking.

"Are you from around here?" Frank asked as we plodded on.

"No — Cardiff actually."

"Not too bad. About an hour or so — am I right?" Frank questioned.

"Yes. I have come here on holiday."

"Oh, we practically live here," Daisy said. "We come often to visit our Aunt. Her house is up the hill a little way along the coast on the way out of Mircove Beach." Frank pointed in the direction of the hill at the other end of the beach.

"Does Mircove not get boring for you?"

"Never!"

"There are always places to explore!" Frank stated enthusiastically.

"Like this one; we're here!" Daisy cried.

 I looked up to see a dark opening in a cliff face.

"Do we go into the cave?" I asked.

"Absolutely not!" Frank looked at my blank expression then laughed. "Of course we do nit-wit!"

I scowled at him. "I knew that."

Daisy and Frank went ahead without displaying any caution or fear. I followed after looking back towards the dwindling light one last time.

"It's dark" I said.

31

"Yes, clever clogs, 'it's dark,' " Frank said imitating me.

"Well if you're so smart, lead the way!" I replied angrily.

"I was already doing that!"

"Anya, Frank!" Daisy snapped. "You've only just met and you're fighting worse than siblings."

I muttered a few curses Mam would have thrashed me severely for as we proceeded deeper into the cave.

I heard water dripping from the top of the cave and some splashed on me; I was very happy for the darkness because it meant Frank or Daisy could not tease me for being scared.

As we got further and further away from the cave entrance it got darker until I could no longer see my hand in front of my face.
I got *really* scared then.

"Maybe we should head back!" I said.   "They're selling ice-cream I think!"

"That's tomorrow," Daisy corrected. "Let's keep going."

So much for heading back. We only stopped when we felt water on our feet.

"Argh!" Frank shouted, nearly jumping out of his skin.
I laughed at him. "Who's pathetic now, scaredy boy!"

"Stop it" Frank snapped.

Daisy knelt down.

"Feel the water," she instructed.

It was warm and smelt clean and fresh, unlike the salty seawater. Wanting to impress, I volunteered to step into the water a little further. It was really deep.

"That's deep," I told them.

I heard Frank fumbling in his pocket and he then said, "I kind of had a match..."

"Idiot!" Daisy shouted at him.

"Sorry."

He struck it and *we* were stuck — stuck for words.

The water glowed an almost turquoise colour and stretched out further than the eye could see. On the walls of the cave were markings, like those Tad had told me prisoners sometimes used to make a tally of the number of days they had spent in captivity. When I looked more closely at the water, I could see *tiny* grey fish swimming merrily about.

"What..."

Daisy and Frank were not impressed. "Seriously?" Frank said disdainfully.

"Rubbish!" Daisy added, kicking the water. "I was hoping for another opening somewhere or something more."

"Rubbish?" I tilted my head. "This is the most interesting thing I've ever seen!"

"Pfft!" Frank scoffed. "There are many more interesting things than this wretched cave."

"We should be going, Frank," Daisy said. "Aunt Jane will be expecting us."

"Where's your moth…" I was about to ask, but Frank made 'stop' gestures at me from behind Daisy.

"Where's your mam's sister," I continued "that's who your aunt is, am I right?"

I wondered what had happened to Daisy and Frank's mother but I dared not ask.

"She's probably sleeping or putting her makeup on — again," Daisy answered dismissively.
Then the light from the match was gone.

"Frank?" I called, looking around. He was gone.

"Frank!" Daisy called anxiously.

"Boo!" Frank shouted, suddenly materialising from nowhere. Daisy and I both jumped. I watched contently as Daisy removed a shoe and struck Frank hard with it.

"Ow. Ow. Ow!" Frank cried in pain.

"Never do that again!" Daisy screamed, nearly crying. "You treat everything as a joke. Someone has already left us — not you too!"
I thought Daisy was overreacting just a *little* but this was not the time or place to say so.

Frank stopped laughing. "Daisy, I'm sorry I…"

"Forget it," Daisy replied, before running off with Frank and me close behind. By the time we were out into the open, the sky was a murky grey and there were fewer people on the beach than when we had entered the cave. I waved to Frank and Daisy and asked if they wanted to play tomorrow.

"No!" Daisy said, rudely.

"Daisy, I did not do anything so don't be nasty to me!" I exclaimed.

She ran off, her curly blonde hair billowing behind her. Frank gave me an apologetic shrug and ran off after his sister.

* * *

I sighed then wandered back over to where my parents had been the last time I had seen them. I spotted Mam and Tad in the distance and walked up to them. Mam turned, saw me and looked like she was about to collapse.

"Anya!" She cried and ran towards me.

I was bewildered. Had I been gone that long? Tad now saw me and hurried over. They hugged me for so long, I had to wriggle my way out of their tight grasp.

"I haven't been gone that long!"

Then Mam did something entirely unexpected — she slapped me across the face. She did not strike me that hard but enough to hurt and bring tears to my eyes. She had never struck me like this before.

I stared at her in shock.

"Where were you?" Tad asked, his words filled with worry.

"Just out with friends..." I muttered.

"Speak up!" he shouted, loud enough for any passers-by to hear.

"I was out with friends!" I shouted back. "I was only behind the rainbow huts and they called me pathetic so I followed them and they're nice but I don't think they have a mam and..."

"Hush!" Mam roared. "You are to go straight to bed, you hear me?"

"Yes, Mam," I muttered.

"Excuse me!"

"Yes Mam," I repeated more loudly.

"Better."

When we arrived back at the B&B, I went straight to bed.

"Your tad and I are going out to watch a show near the beach. We will be back shortly."

"Do not leave the room," Tad instructed as they left.

I thought about how I so wanted to play out with Daisy and Frank again — even though they could have been a bit nicer — and how Mam had slapped me. I felt my cheek. It still stung a little. I opened up my leather case and took out *The Red Fairy Book* I've had since I was four. Even at eleven, I could not help but read it over and over again. A couple of fairy tale stories later, I heard Tad turn the key in the lock. I hid the book under my pillow and shut my eyes tight, pretending to snore lightly. I felt Mam's soft breath on me and for a moment I thought she knew I was awake, but she moved away and I sighed quietly, feeling relieved. Eventually, I fell asleep and dreamt I was running aimlessly through a field of endless green. It had no start or end and I kept running, not knowing who I was.

Three

Ice Creams And a Market

"Argh!" I jumped out of bed as I felt something cold on my face.

Tad laughed — "Got you!"

I moaned, "Tad!"

Mam entered the room, already dressed.

"Where've you been?" I asked, rubbing my crusty eyes.

"The wash huts. It's quite a long walk to get there but your father can take you whilst I tell them to start getting our breakfast ready. Apparently, breakfast takes a while to cook."

"Anya, are you ready?" Tad asked

"Hardly. Where's my soap?"

"Got it," he replied "Lets go."

As Mam had mentioned, the journey to the wash house from the B&B was a small trek. We walked along the sandy pathways barefoot, letting the golden dust sink in between our toes. It felt wonderful.

"Your mam is still cross about yesterday," he said after a while.

"I can tell."

"Well it was very insensitive of you to go running off with strangers; and, you were gone for three hours!"

"Three! And in any case, they're not strangers, they're friends," I said defiantly.

"Have you met them before?"

"Well no…"

"Seen them?"

"No, but…"

"Do you see my point? Your mam and I were extremely worried! Next time you intend to do something like that, at least tell us where you're going."

I nodded, my eyes downcast.

"Oh look, we've arrived," he said.

The showers were open — as in *no* curtains or cubicles!

"No way!" I shouted.

"I'm not feeling too enthusiastic either," Tad exclaimed. "I will have breakfast without washing!"

"I mean no offence Anya, but — you smell!" Tad proclaimed, laughing loudly.

39

"I do not!" I protested, glaring at him.

In the end, I had no choice but to shower. Luckily, the male and female sections were separated! There were two women and a small girl already showering; one of the ladies was so plump she had fold upon fold of skin! Hesitating at first, I took off my clothes, wondering how Tad was coping with the other men.

"Brrrrr!" I exclaimed loudly — the water in the showers was freezing! Where was the hot water? I looked at the two women and the girl who seemed to be enjoying their showers as much as I was hating mine!

I decided I would get my shower over and done with as quickly as possible — especially as I could not wait for breakfast — so I started to lather and then apply my soap. I felt extremely uncomfortable as the plump woman was right next to me and hogging all my shower space. To make matters worse, I got some soap in my eyes which caused them to sting a little, but at least it took my mind off the awkwardness. Once I had rinsed off the soap, I grabbed my towel and dried as quickly as I could, pulled on the clothes Tad had brought for me, and dashed out of the washroom.

"Phew!"

Tad was waiting for me outside. "How was it?" he asked. Looking intently at my face he voiced his own opinion. "Not so good, I'm guessing!"

"And yours?" I asked.

"Glorious! No one else was in there!"

"You lucky thing. Race you to the B&B!" I said dashing away.

We ran laughing together until we reached the B&B, almost out of breath.

"I won," I panted.

We both found and joined Mam, who had saved us a table. Our mouth-watering breakfast was laid out for us and we sat down eagerly to satisfy our hunger.

"Napkin!" Mam instructed.

I groaned but did as she asked. My breakfast was comprised of three rashers of crispy bacon, pancakes — a rare treat — apple slices and a glass of orange juice.

"Yum! Thanks, Mam!"

She smiled at me. I suspected I had been forgiven. I tend to look around the room when I eat, and in doing so I spotted Daisy and Frank, sat with their aunt. Frank saw me too and waved, as did Daisy who probably felt bad for being so rude to me the day before. I wondered why they were at the B&B when they had a house of their own along the coast where they were staying with their aunt.

Two old ladies were sat at a table next to theirs, drinking tea and munching biscuits — just like my Mam-gu would do.

There was a large family of seven crammed around a table meant for five, and I counted three boys, two girls and their mother and father.

Betsy was going from table to table carrying plates of mouth-watering breakfast, as was a young man and a young woman, who I guessed must have been workers at the B&B.

"That was delightful," I said, my tummy full.

"I know," she replied.

"So Mam — can I go and play with Daisy and Frank?"

"Who?"

"Those two children over there," I indicated, motioning with my eyes.

"No."

"Why not?"

"Because I said so."

"At least talk to their mother, Maria," Tad whispered, helping me out.

"It's their aunt actually, but go on Mam, they are alright."

"Oh, alright then!" Mam conceded with a small huff.

She walked delicately over to Daisy and Frank's table and stood there talking to their aunt for a while, looking happy enough.

"They *seem to be* lovely people!" she declared as she walked back to us.

I held my breath.

"So, you may go and play with them — as long as you tell us where you're going first!"

"Thank you ever so much Mam!"

I hugged her tightly then waved Frank and Daisy over. Daisy and Frank smiled and came across to me.

"We'll only go as far as the market Mrs Rees," Daisy told Mam.

"Have fun!" Tad called as we ran out of the dining room.

* * *

"Aunt Jane treated us to a B&B breakfast," Daisy said.

"And look, I've got one shilling!" she bragged, waving it about as she skipped along the beach.

"Well you ought to be careful with it Dais, or someone's bound to steal it," Frank warned.

"What do you know about money?"

"I'm just warning you, that's all."

"Well don't!" she shouted

"Why are you always so upset, Daisy. I'm only trying to look out for you!"

"Go away!" Daisy flounced off then stopped and turned to me. "Anya? Are you coming?"

I did not want to choose between Frank and Daisy but Frank had already turned on his heels and was walking away so I followed Daisy, running to keep up.

"He's a nuisance."

I rather thought Daisy was the nuisance, not Frank, but I kept quiet not wanting to upset her.

"What shall we do?" I asked after we had walked a short distance across the sand.

"How about ice-creams?"

"Sounds lovely but I don't have any money," I said mournfully.

"I'll buy you one, silly!" Daisy said laughing as she pulled me along to the back of the ice-cream line. I wondered how Daisy had come to possess a shilling, but I soon abandoned this thought as the lure of ice cream was too great.

While we waited, I looked at what Daisy was wearing today — a loose, green gown, and she had tied a green ribbon in her hair.

"Wow. Lots of people like ice-cream!" I exclaimed as we stood behind a lady and her son who appeared to be about three years of age.

"They sure do. You're lucky though."

"Why?" I questioned.

"Because the line is usually ten times longer than this!"

We laughed together and she shared with me what it was like to live so close to Mircove Beach.

"What should we do?"

"Can we go to the market after our ice-creams?"

I thought the idea of a market boring. I thought this one might be like the ones in Cardiff I had been to ages ago; however, I did not want to upset Daisy as we'd just become friends, so I agreed.

We finally got to the front of the line for our ice creams and I contemplated the delicious-sounding flavours.

"They all look like angels have made them!" I gushed. "Should I go for chocolate, vanilla or raspberry?"

They all looked SO good!

"I'll order mine while you think about what you would like to choose," Daisy said. "I'll have my usual please," Daisy said to the ice cream man.

I opted for the raspberry cone, copying Daisy, as hers looked amazing. I clapped eyes properly on the ice cream server. The man was old and his back was hunched but he smiled as he scooped up Daisy's ice cream. His hair was dotted about his head in little patches, he had a crooked nose and his eyes were most striking — a stormy blue. He was wearing a white shirt which contrasted with his ice cream covered, blue apron.

"Strawberry swirl coming right up, Miss Lane."

He turned around and fumbled through a big, white box which had frost creeping up its sides.

"What's that?" I asked Daisy.

"A cooler. Haven't you seen a cooler before?" I shook my head.

"Oh. Well, it's where Mr Robin keeps his ice creams. The cooler keeps them cold and fresh."

I watched as Mr Robin pulled a tub of ice cream out from the cooler which read "Strawberry Swirl" on the side.

Mr Robin was definitely taking his time. Not that he appeared to have much left!

I whispered to Daisy, "He's a bit slow, isn't he?"

"Yes, but Mr Robin's a dear old thing, however old and slow he might be," she whispered back in his defence.

"Here you are, Daisy, and who is this may I ask?"

"I am well, thank you, Mr Robin. This is my new friend, Anya. She's here on holiday for a few days."

"Well, welcome to Mircove missy. Now, what can I get you?"

"Please may I have a raspberry cone?"

"Of course, my lovely."

While waiting, I watched transfixed as Daisy licked her ice cream, intently occupied by its creamy goodness.

"Here we are!" Mr Robin announced, handing me my ice cream.

"Thank you!" I said, almost snatching it from his hand.

"Somebody's eager!" Daisy declared, chuckling.

I finished my raspberry ice cream so quickly I regretted doing so, soon wanting more.

Daisy placed her shilling on the counter and said to Mr Robin, "That'll be sixpence and tuppence please."

"Miss hoity-toity! Here you are cheesecake!"

I would hate to be called cheesecake but Daisy did not seem to mind.

"How about another scoop?" I ventured daringly but, to my disappointment, Daisy simply smiled at me.

"Why don't we go to the market?"

"Okay."

Staying put to eat more ice cream seemed a much better idea, but I followed Daisy dutifully as she walked in the opposite direction to Mr Robin the ice cream man.

* * *

The sand soon turned into cobble as we walked along the pathway. Seagulls screeched above us in the clear, blue sky. Children skipped about on the beach behind us as some adults sunbathed whilst others strolled lazily along shaded by umbrellas.

"Welcome to the market!"

It was nothing like Splott Road market with stalls dotted everywhere and people shouting. Rather, it was a tranquil and civilised environment where people could buy things without their ears being assaulted by the shouts of a nearby stall owner. Instead of stalls, Mircove had little shops on either side of the cobbled street so you could enter and leave each shop with ease.

I spotted the toyshop and my heart leapt.

"Oh, please can we go in there!" I gushed.

"I had the same idea." We skipped arm in arm, to the toyshop. The shop bell gave a loud *'ring-ding-ding'* as we entered, causing me to jump with surprise. I must confess I felt rather silly because I had even given a little yelp, which Daisy clearly found grounds for hysterical laughter at my expense.

"Morning, Daisy — and who is this?" the woman behind the counter asked.

The woman wore a short, garnet dress with buttons down the front. Although the dress showed rather a lot of leg, which Mam would not have approved of, the woman had at least styled it well.

Her figure was curvy, unlike mine, so the dress looked wonderful. Her hair was chocolate-brown and it hung loosely around her shoulders.

"She's..."

"I'm Anya and I'm from Cardiff. I'm here on holiday."

"How delightful! Mircove is a beautiful place which I'm sure you have found out already," the woman said.

"May we have a look at the toys, Lilian?" Daisy asked. "I know all of them but Anya hasn't been here before of course."

"Go right ahead, girls!"

I walked slowly around the tiny shop, transfixed by all I saw. The shop walls were crimson red and the floor was a polished wood which had seen countless years of use.

Displayed on shelves were mini china dolls in cardboard boxes, each filled with tissue paper to keep them safe. There were also multi-coloured hoops propped against a wall, beside which was an army of toy farm animals on a small counter. I picked up and closely examined a miniature sheep and lamb, a cow and her two calves, some pigs and a brown stallion. My goodness — there were so many things! Tea sets, pull-along horses, big dolls and small dolls dressed in the finest dresses with matching bows in their hair, rubber balls and glass marbles in sacks, and countless jigsaws.

"Why is everything in Mircove so difficult to choose from!" I wailed.

I could not decide between a doll with beautiful blonde hair who was wearing a pink dress with a bow, or a blue hoop. I so wanted to boast to Annis and Sioned that *I too* had a hoop, so I decided to buy it.

"I have chosen."

"Me too," Daisy chirped in.

We went to the main counter to pay.

"How much for a hoop and marbles please Lilian?" Daisy enquired.

"Let's see — one shilling."

"One shilling!" I cried, "That's expensive!"

"Hmm — well just this once I'll reduce the price as this is your first visit to Mircove young lady."

"Oh thank you ever so much!"

"Think nothing of it. Oh, and if anyone asks, you paid a shilling — alright?"

We nodded and Daisy gave Lilian sixpence. I was pleased Daisy had bought me a toy, but to be honest, the hoop wasn't much fun.

"Here, like this," Daisy instructed as she attempted to show me how to spin the hoop on my waist and arm; however, I was hopeless and the hoop kept dropping from my waist after barely a spin and when it was on my arm it hung limp and I could not get it to spin.

"There's no point," I sighed dejectedly.

"Yes, there is. Look."

Daisy once again attempted to teach me but to no avail — I remained woefully incapable!

I was angry I had let my envy of Annis and Sioned interfere with my decisions.

"Cheer up!" said Daisy, noticing my miserable face. "We can go and watch the Punch and Judy puppet show — they always have it showing!"

Daisy led me across the cobblestones to the end of the market where a large red tent stood. From inside, I could hear children laughing with joy, women gossiping and men shouting and larking around boisterously. As we entered, I saw blankets on the floor and rows and rows of chairs. To my left, people were selling gingerbread and enticing hot chocolate drinks.

"That smells positively delightful!" I cried. "Daisy, let's get some drinks and gingerbread."

"Alright but I do not have much money left and my aunt doesn't want me to spend it all."

"Oh."

"Not to worry, I've got a plan. Follow my lead."

Daisy took my hand and led me past the bustling crowd of people watching the comedy routine taking place on the stage. The comedian was extremely short — the height of a boy and only reaching the level of my waist — but his face was that of a man. He was wearing a black waistcoat, black trousers, a musty yellow shirt and red tie.

I thought he looked ridiculous and his jokes seemed like nonsense to me, but the audience appears to be enjoying it immensely!

"Come on!" Daisy whispered to me. She led me to the front of the gingerbread queue and said, "When I say go, nick a gingerbread."

"Nick?"

"It means steal genius!" Daisy said, laughing. "Grab one."

"Oh."

How could I steal? My parents had raised me to be a well-mannered, honest girl and now I was contemplating theft?

"I don't think I can," I confessed.

"We won't get into any trouble and besides it's not really stealing if they have so many — they would not miss two."

I wasn't sure but agreed hesitantly.

"One, two, three GO!"

Daisy grabbed a gingerbread man with an icing mouth and jelly drop buttons and I grabbed a little bunny with a liquorice nose. Then we ran.

"Oi!"

"Oh no!"

That was what I feared — someone had spotted us in the act of stealing!

Four

The Right Thing - I Think

*I*started to turn around, ready to accept my fate but Daisy yanked me out of the tent and shoved me behind it

"We have to own up," I panted.

"Never!"

"Why?" I asked.

"We just can't. I'm already in enough trouble…"

I was going to ask her what she meant but we heard the man's angry shouting, so we dashed off. Finally, after what seemed like endless running Daisy and I crashed down behind the building next to the B&B.

"What if my parents see me?" I asked.

"Shh!"

Daisy held her finger to her lips for several moments before telling me the man was off our trail.

"This doesn't feel right," I confessed.   "Yes, it does; you'll be fine!

54

The thought of what Mam and Tad would say gave me the shivers. They were angry enough with me spending a couple of hours with Daisy up the beach. How furious would they be now? My breath quickened which made me clutch at my chest.

"What's wrong?" Daisy asked worriedly.

"I — can't — breathe!"

"I'll get you some water. At least I'll be sure to do it without getting caught."

"No. I'll do it," I wheezed.

My heart was beating so rapidly, I thought my chest would burst. Standing up with as much dignity as I could muster, I walked around the corner from our hiding spot. I found a tap and wrapped my lips around the cold metal tube. I needed that water. Halfway back to where Daisy was, I stopped. This didn't feel right at all and nothing Daisy said would change that. I decided to do what was right; I turned around and walked in the opposite direction.

"Hello, Sir."

"Hello, Miss. Hey — have I seen you befor...

"Sir, I have come to apologise. I stole from your stall but it was only because I was scared and anxious and I had only just made a new friend. Please don't be angry but if you want, you can lock me up."

To my surprise, he just chuckled and said, "Have it for free! I am not in the least pleased about you two stealing my goods but at least you owned up. Where is the other young miss? Did she not think to do the same? And what is her name?"

I was so pleased and relieved, I told him, and ran back down to where Daisy was hiding, beaming from ear to ear.

"That water must have been plenty good to make you grin like a Cheshire!" She chuckled.

I sat down beside her.

"So, what now?" I asked.

She was writing her name in the sand with a twig. "I better get going. Aunty will be waiting for me; so will Frank."

I waved as she got up and walked back along the beach. I found Mam and Tad sat in front of the B&B tucking into sandwiches.

"Hello!" I called, running up to them.

"Hello, my dear!" said Tad, smiling.

"Did you have fun?" Mam asked.

Before having a chance to answer, I spotted Daisy running towards us.

"Hello, Daisy!" I shouted.

She stopped a little distance away, beckoned me over and then retreated to the side of the B&B. Running towards her, I could see she looked worried.

"What's the matter?" I asked. She pressed her lips together and stared at the ground.

"Daisy?" I placed my hand on her shoulder, but she pulled away quickly.

"I know what you did," she muttered. "You told him and now all of them are searching for me."

"Who?" I asked.

"The people at the market you idiot!"

It finally hit me that somehow, she had found out I had told the man in the big tent she was the one who stole.

"Oh no…"

"Oh yes! And now I'm in huge trouble because this isn't the first time I've stolen from there!"

"I'm so sorry I…"

"Save it."

A tear trailed down Daisy's cheek and she quickly wiped it away. Then she turned on her heel and fled back down the beach.

I felt awful. That she was a petty thief didn't sit well with me and neither would it sit well with Tad and Mam, but I had just lost my only friend here at Mircove. The thought of what I was now going to do in Mircove for the next few days without friends to play with stayed with me and kept me wondering for a while.

Walking back, I felt too tired to have lunch. Tad was now sitting in the front room in deep conversation with a familiar man.

"Tad?"

"Oh hello, Anya. This is the man you saw painting, Mr Linkman."

"How do you do?" Mr Linkman shook my hand.

"You'll make a fine painter yet," he said.

"How about some tips for you, aye?"

I couldn't resist, so I sat down.

"First you must paint your background wash. That way, if you do make a mistake, you won't be likely to muck up the foreground object. Make sure you paint from dark to light colours."

"Thank you Mr Linkmann," I gushed, all the while itching to talk to Tad.

"And the best tip of all, young lady, is to blend your colours in. Paint the first colour in broad strokes, and then without rinsing your brush, dip it into the second colour and paint in long strokes along the edge of the first colour to create the blend.

"Does that help?" He asked with a smile.

"Oh absolutely, I can't wait to try them out."

"Tad can I please speak to you?"

"Of course, darling. One minute Mr Linkman..."

"What is it?" Tad asked me.

"Well let's say, hypothetically, if a person did something bad like, say steal and they did it with another person, but they owned up afterwards. Was owning up the right thing?"

"Well, Anya, if you think it was the right thing, then yes."

"But it was not m..." I tried to say but Tad interrupted me.

"I know that person was you, Anya." His tone was grave.

"I didn't want to Tad but Daisy thought it was a bit of harmless fun. Can we please not tell Mam. I don't want her to get any more upset."

"Well, I am shocked and so disappointed, Anya. My own honest, hardworking, kind child stealing? It doesn't make sense." The disappointment in Tad's voice was crushing.

"I *am* sorry."

He lowered himself and brought his face close to mine. "If you ever do anything like that again, Anya..." I didn't want to know what Tad would do to me.

"One last thing, Anya Rees. I never want you speaking to that treacherous girl Daisy again. Am I clear?"

I gasped. "But she's my..."

"Am I clear?" Tad repeated.

"Yes Tad," I grumbled.

"Good. Now I won't tell your mam as long as you are going to promise never to do anything like that ever again."

"I promise Tad."

"That is all I can ask for," Tad said.

"Now, your mam was wondering if you wanted to go into the bathing huts with her. Men are not allowed, unfortunately, or I would have joined you. We'll finish off with Mr Linkmann then and we'll be on our way."

"Oh, yes please!" I exclaimed, perking up at the thought of riding in a hut across the sea.

* * *

We found Mam reclining on a deck chair. She was writing some sort of letter and I thought I saw a flash of my name but she hid it away quickly.

"You gave me a fright, Anya."

"Sorry," I said, apologising, "but Tad said you wanted us to go down to the bathing hut."

"Come on then," she said as she stood up brushing some sand off.

Tad watched from the beach as we paid for a bathing machine. The machine was wooden with number 004 imprinted on it. It had four huge wheels, two on either side. A beautiful, brown stallion pulled it.

"Look at that horse!" I gasped.

"I know, it's so handsome," Mam agreed.

As we walked into the hut I began to feel less excited. "Why on earth is it wobbling?" I looked worriedly down at the floor.

"We're in the sea, Anya."

"That would make sense." I weighed out the chances of me drowning or staying alive. Fifty-fifty. I didn't like it.

A man slapped the horse's behind, and the stallion started to trot into the water. I swayed from side to side.

"I'm going to be sick," I said, bending over and clutching my stomach.

"Anya," Mam laughed, "We've hardly left the beach."

Soon enough, the horse had pulled us fairly far out into the sea. Mam chucked my bathing suit at me, telling me to put it on. She already had hers on underneath her dress.

"Here's the fun part," Mam said.

"What. There's more?" I blinked regretting my decision to come into this death trap in the first place.

"Well yes," she answered, "now, I'm going to go first."

"To do what?"

"Jump in, you na-na," she said chuckling.

61

I stared at her. "Pardon me."

"Jump in Anya," she repeated, "it's not that bad."

"No way!" I stated.

"No!"

"Hold my hand."

I gripped her hand with such vigour my own hand was turning bright red.

"Now, when I get to three, we jump in. One, two, three." Having little choice, I jumped into the cold, salty water. When I came back up to the surface, I was freezing. "Cold. So cold," I stammered, my teeth clattering.

"Swim about," Mam advised, "You'll get warmer."

I tried to swim about forgetting I couldn't swim that well. This was nothing like messing around in the shallow end of Cardiff docks.

"Help! I'm drowning!" I flapped my arms about in the water and kicked my legs desperately.

"Anya — put your feet down."

"Oh, right." I put my feet on the sandy floor, embarrassed. I insisted on going back to the shore. That was enough beach for one day.

Five

Just My Luck - More Trouble. Grave Trouble

⟨~⟩

The next couple of days at Mircove Beach went surprisingly quickly. I tried not to think about the loss of a playmate. Mam and I visited the market for some satin fabric and accessories for the house. To pass the time, Tad had befriended some holidaying men whom he got on with like a house on fire. The day before we left Mircove Beach was my twelfth birthday. It was excellently celebrated. Betsy made a very special cake which read 'Happy Birthday Anya' in white icing. I found out the letter Mam had been writing on the beach was for my better day. Another one for my collection of letters from Mam. For presents, I got a new dress, not the frilly, posh sort but a nice loose, cotton one with buttons down the front. I also got the delightful novel *Jane Eyre*, by Charlotte Bronte, which I tucked into straight away.

* * *

Much to everyone's dismay, the day of departure eventually came. I desperately wanted to say good-bye to Daisy and Frank; they had made my time here fun, but the best I could do, was wish it. Tad had made his feelings clear on that score. I wished I'd spent more time using some of Mr Linkman's tips to paint but time moves swiftly when you're having fun and, in other words, I had completely forgotten.

The day was mostly a lazy one with a beach walk and then back to the B&B to pack our things. It was late afternoon when Mam called to me say, "Anya, grab your things. The carriage is here."

Tad hauled his own case plus all of Mam's extra bags filled with dresses and makeup which she never got to use here but wouldn't let me anywhere near.

The carriage man who brought us to Mircove Beach was waiting patiently. When we'd finished loading our cases, he clicked his tongue and the horse broke into a steady trot.

As we rounded the hill up from the beach, I saw Daisy and Frank out the front of a quaint looking white cottage. I thought that it must've been their aunt's cottage. I waved sheepishly. Frank half waved back while Daisy just stared until we rode out of sight.

After a while, Mam said, "I really wish we could've spent more time together. You know, as a family."

Without looking up from the Mircove Paper he was reading Tad replied, "I think it was fine."

"I agree." I shared. "Sometimes we need to make new friends or be by ourselves. I really had fun."

"Well, that's all that matters, but we still could've have taken some family photos," Mam continued.

"Maria!" Tad moaned.

"What?" Mam asked, "Photos make for great memories."

"I don't disagree, Maria, but I could think of better ways of spending my time than going to some photo booth to take photos in which I would look like an idiot in a straitjacket."

"Ok, ok," I said, "Let's all just calm down."

"To be fair I had a great time at the market," Mam admitted. "I found a lovely sale where I bought you some new dresses, Anya."

The carriage man seized the opportunity to strike up a conversation. This man could talk the hind legs off a donkey! Remembering Mam had packed some lunch, I opened my carrier and devoured my ham sandwich. Soon, I grew tired of the man's nattering so I rested my head on the cool, carriage glass and drifted off to sleep.

"My hoop!" I gasped, suddenly waking up remembering as I was jolted sideways. It looked quite late and there were a few stars dotted around the sky. The moon was nowhere to be seen.

"What honey? Well, we're nearly home." Mam seemed to have been writing another note. Soon, the carriage drew to a halt outside the house. "Come and get your case from the back," Mam requested.

"But my hoop! I left my hoop — oh please can we go back?"

"What? Of course we can't go back, that would be ridiculous. Plus, its school tomorrow."

"But I so badly want to show Annis and Sioned my hoop. They won't believe me otherwise."

"Well, I think they are terrible friends then. They cause you nothing but trouble," she snapped. "Now will you please get your case?"

I huffed all the way to the house. I threw my shoes off and took my case upstairs. Feeling too tired to unpack my things, I flopped onto my bed and painted. I painted peaceful picturesque hills but instead of clear, blue skies above it, I contrasted the hills with a huge thunderstorm with big lightning bolts and heavy rain. Satisfied that it sufficiently reflected my mood, I set my paints and brushes down and fell into a fitful sleep.

* * *

I woke up far too early but decided to get ready for school anyway. Trudging to the bathroom, I washed my face and brushed my teeth in the simple sink against the sidewall, all the while looking in the oval mirror on the wall to make sure my smile was clean. Opposite the sink was the toilet which is enough said. On the back wall of the bathroom stood the bathtub with silver taps. I washed and put on my school uniform before heading downstairs for breakfast.

Being so early, Mam hadn't made me any food so I made do with a slice of bread smeared with the last of the strawberry jam.

"Well you're early," Tad called as he came downstairs. "Your mam's not feeling a hundred percent so I'll be walking you to school today. Good thing you're early."

He went to make himself a jam sandwich. "Who finished the jam? That was for my breakfast!"

Tad turned slowly towards me, "ANYA!" He made a dive for me and we ended up rolling around on the floor, giggling.

"Come on then, we better go.

I stuffed the remnants of my breakfast down my throat, washed it all down with a glass of water and quickly dashed upstairs to see Mam.

"Are we ready?" Tad asked as I got back down. Nodding, we headed out for school.

"Have a wonderful day," Tad called as he saw me off at the gate.

"You too."

Annis and Sioned were playing with their hoops when I ran over. They shared a quick look of distaste. I wondered to myself as I often did, why I called them my friends.

"Annis, Sioned!" I called excitedly, jogging over to them.

"Um — hello," Sioned said, looking awkward.

"I went to Mircove!"

"No, you did not," Annis snorted.

"Yes, I did," I replied indignantly.

"Prove it," Sioned said.

"I — I can't at the moment. But I did have a hoop — just like your one."

"Pathetic," Annis scoffed and they both laughed in unison.

Then I did the unexpected. I was sick of their mean ways. They had never once been nice to me, but I insisted on tagging along behind them like a tail. I had had enough. I slapped Annis then kicked Sioned. They both stared at me in shock. Annis sat on the ground and Sioned followed suit. They wailed like babies.

I was out of luck. At that precise moment, Mrs Juper, our poetry teacher, stepped out onto the playground.

"Anya slapped me so hard, I'm nearly bleeding," Annis wailed to Mrs Juper, covering the cheek I'd hit.

"And she kicked *me* so hard my leg buckled and my bone nearly broke," Sioned added.

At that precise moment, the blessed school bell rang. Well, it seemed blessed at the time. Rushing into school, my eyes stinging, I hid in the toilets. I sobbed and sobbed until Mrs Juper came in.

She knocked on my cubicle door. "Anya? Anya Rees, do let me in this instant!"

I made weeing sounds, "Sssssss…"

"Anya, I'm not stupid; I know you're not using the toilet." Slowly, I opened the door to reveal a very cross looking teacher.

"Now, what you did to Annis and Sioned was not acceptable. You know, in this school, we do not abide bullying."

"Bullying?" I questioned, astonished. "No! I slapped Annis but it was really just a brush and Sioned, I barely touched her."

"Yes, *bull-y-ing*," Mrs Juper repeated as if she was explaining it to a lunatic. "They told me you've been very unkind to them these past few weeks."

"No! It's the other way around." but Mrs Juper just shook her head. It seemed her mind was made up.

"Lying is also intolerable. I have no choice but to keep you in after school and to make you write sorry letters to both Annis and Sioned. I expect you to be in class in five minutes."

I was livid. First day back from holiday and now I was getting in trouble. And apparently, I'd bullied them!

As furious and outraged as I was, I had to compose myself. There was no way I was giving them the pleasure of seeing how much they had affected me. Washing my face, I walked into the classroom with the last dregs of dignity I could muster.

"Sit next to Layla," Mrs Juper ordered.

I did as I was told. Layla was a shy girl with curly, ginger hair and piercing green eyes. She always hung her head and hardly ever spoke. At least she wouldn't bother me if she was naturally quiet.

I willed the day to go slowly, but it passed rapidly and before I knew it, I was walking to the far end of the school where you were kept if you misbehaved. Tad would be so cross. He would have been turned back when he came for me. The room had chalk and crayon drawings around the walls. The paint was peeling off and there were cracks in the ceiling. There were desks with rickety wooden chairs and broken table legs. I sat down at the one which looked the most stable.

Mr Ball, the Geography teacher, came into the classroom. This was going to be hard! There was no-nonsense and there was Mr Ball. He was followed by three boys and a girl: Simon, Oliver, Benjamin and Sunita. They were siblings whose family had moved to Cardiff from India. Their tad had been a wealthy man in British India I heard. Stories had gone around that they had a grand house with sugar cane farms, hosts of servants and bellboys. Apparently, they belonged to a class known as 'Pukka Sahib' which meant 'first-class' or similar. But that was British India. This was Cardiff. They were forever getting into trouble and that's how I and everyone at school knew them. Hardly first class, in my opinion. They just couldn't seem to grasp life in humble Cardiff or the school rules yet.

"Simon sit there, Sunita you there, Oliver next to Anya and Benjamin over here," Mr Ball instructed. "Silence, please. I will be back shortly. Anyone caught talking stays in here for an extra hour."

71

As soon as Mr Ball left the room, the siblings started *nattering*.

"So what are you in here for. It is normally just us." Oliver asked.

"Well, I kind of kicked and slapped some girls but it wasn't hard at all. Then they claimed I was bullying them. I am so sick of them. What about you?"

Sunita, who's a year older than me said, "I am in here because I gave the teacher an apple. It was rotten but how was I supposed to know?"

The siblings laughed then Oliver said, "I am in here because I said some rude words. George Harrison told me to say them and he said the teacher would be happy."

"That's horrible," I replied, "I hate George Harrison." Oliver nodded. If he didn't feel that way about George Harrison before, he certainly did now.

Benjamin confessed, "I am in here because I ripped up my Arithmetic book. It is not only boring, but it's hard, too. The ones in India are fun." He was five years younger than me, the baby of them all but no less trouble.

"And last but not least me," said Simon who is two years older than me, "I am in here because I punched a guy called Neil Strong. He was getting on my nervous system. Now he's got a black eye." He said the last part almost proudly.

"It's called *nerves* brother. He's getting on your *nerves*," Sunita corrected.

Simon rolled his eyes.

"I heard talking." Mr Ball came back into the room carrying a stack of paper and a pot of pencils.

"Who was talking?"

"It was me," Sunita owned up.

"And me," Oliver said.

"And me," Simon joined.

"And me!" Benjamin piped up.

"Well, it can't always be all of you talking but very well, you will all suffer another hour," Mr Ball said. "Apart from you Anya."

It must be so nice to have siblings. Someone to stick up for you, play with you and keep you company. I wish I had one.

"Anya, come and hand out some paper and pencils." I got the paper and pencils and handed them out.

"Now, each of you will write an apology letter to who you are sorry to. Simon, you will write one to Neil, Benjamin, to Mrs Slurr, Sunita, to Mr Shorl, and Oliver one to Mrs Plum *and* George Harrison."

"Why George?" Oliver asked.

"Do not interrupt me, boy," Mr Ball fumed.

"You blamed him for something he did not do."

"He *did* tell me to say those words though."

"One more peep and I will keep *all* of you in for yet another hour. You lot already have one added on so I suggest you keep that little mouth shut."

"As I was saying before I was rudely interrupted," he said, glaring at Oliver, "Oliver, you will be writing two letters and Anya, you will be writing two as well. One to Annis and one to Sioned."

I groaned quietly. Mam was right. I needed better friends.

"What are you waiting for? On with it!"

Eventually, I came up with:

To Annis
   Sorry for slapping you. Very, very *softly.*
From Anya.

My letter to Sioned was very similar.

To Sioned
   Sorry for kicking you. Very, very *softly.*
From Anya.

I handed my letters to Mr Ball. He shook his head disapprovingly but to my luck didn't say anything. The rest of the time I was sat in the dull classroom, I was insufferably bored. In the end, I decided to think of ways to get Sioned and Annis back.

I could:

1. Pop a frog in one of their satchels
2. Throw eggs at them
3. Spread rumours about them
4. Throw their hoops in a river.

Number four appealed to me most but I knew I wasn't really going to do it unless I wanted another telling-off.

"You may go," Mr Ball opened the door and I charged out. I felt bad for my new 'friends' and I waved at them just as Mr Ball slammed the door shut. I could hear him shouting. Mam was waiting outside for me. I was thankful she felt better enough to come for me but the look on her face said it all.

"Mam, it wasn't…"

"We'll talk about it with your father."

The walk home was extremely awkward and as I got into the house, I tried to dash upstairs but Tad said, "Hold it!"

Sighing, I walked into the kitchen.

"You do know what you did was very wrong, don't you?" he asked.

"Yes," I answered head bowed.

"Sorry?"

"Yes, Tad."

"What's got into you these days, Anya. First the episode in Mircove, now this?"

I could have fainted but thankfully Mam had just wandered into the hallway out of earshot.

"And you'll never do it again?"

"Yes, Tad," I replied, wanting this to be over so badly.

"Good. Now, go and wash and when you come down you can have some dinner."

Entering the room Mam looked rather unimpressed with me for only receiving a warning, but she left the matter alone.

Six

All Families Get Together - at Some Point

Thankfully, it wasn't a full week at school. The events of my first day back from holiday left a sour taste in my mouth. I couldn't wait for Friday, so I did my best to keep out of Annis's and Sioned's way for the next two days.

Frankly, it did me good. It made for a quieter life. I didn't have to be subjected to their meanness. What did I ever see in a friendship with them I wondered?

I heard Tad's rapping on my door.

"Anya, time to get ready."

"Tad!" I groaned. "It's not school today, can I just have a lazy day?"

"You would have had to get ready anyway," Tad responded.

77

"Why?"

"Have you forgotten — we're going to a family gathering at your mam-gu's? It's your cousin Jemima's first Holy Communion. So you'd better put something smart on. At least we're not going to the church service. It would be have been a much longer day then."

I hated family gatherings. Aunties and uncles fussing over you, cousins sneering at you because you didn't have the latest, most fashionable frock. It was dreadful!

"You know, Tad. It may be easier if I didn't go," I said carefully, "I might ruin your fun."

"If I've got to put up with it, so do you, Anya," Tad said. He wasn't very fond of my Mam's mam or family gatherings either.

Sighing exasperatedly, I got cleaned up and put on my dusty-rose coloured dress. It had *far* too many ruffles for my liking, but Mam-gu loved it so, so it would have to do. Wrapping my cotton shawl around my shoulders, I headed downstairs to polish my high button leather boots.

"Isn't Mam coming?" I asked Tad as we met in the corridor. He was all dressed up in a black jacket, waistcoat, black trousers and top hat.

"I am afraid not," he replied. "She's not feeling too great so I thought it best if she had a lie-in. We'll have to endure this."

A worried look crossed his face, but he quickly exchanged it with a smile.

"She'll be fine."

A few moments later, Tad returned with some tea for Mam. I followed him in to see her. It was clear to see why he had looked worried. She looked drawn and a bit grey. Seeing me, Mam faked a smile.

"Bore da, my love."

"Bore da Mam."

"I should stay back with you."

"No No sweet pea. Your Mam-gu will not be pleased if neither of us turned up."

She had a point. But it did nothing to soothe my worry. Heading for the bathroom, I tried desperately to do my hair up in a fancy way instead of leaving it to drape down like a hood, but my attempts were fruitless. I didn't want to disturb Mam, so I kept trying until I got something like a lopsided bird's nest. I really did not have the energy or will to redo it, so I decided to let it be.

The two-mile-long walk to Mam-gu's was a brisk and mostly quiet one. Each of us was worrying about Mam in our own way. It was very busy, what with the carriages and the traders in Splott market. I very nearly got distracted by a stall selling books, but Tad gently led me away promising we would come back another time. Outside Mam-gu's, we could already hear the ruckus going on inside.

We looked at each other in despair before walking through her grand doors.

"Welcome my darling." I was nearly squeezed to death by strong, familiar arms.

"Mam-gu!" I smiled, hugging her back.
She still had her knitted red shawl and tall black hat on. Seemed they hadn't been home long from the service.

"Come on in."

"Hello," Tad said to Mam-gu.

"Nice to see you," she replied.

"Ble mae dy fam? Mam-gu insisted on speaking as much Welsh as she could to me.

"She had to give this a miss. She's not been feeling too great lately," Tad answered.
"Hmm."

She walked back into the parlour and I turned to Tad and asked, "Why are you and Mam-gu so — tense with each other."

"Well, I guess she's never liked me. She didn't think me fit to marry your mam, but I did and here we are."

I still didn't get why they were both so preoccupied with the past, but I didn't argue with Tad.

"Go and have some fun, Anya, I'll meet you in the dining hall later." Walking away, Tad cried out "Eddie! Is that you, boyo?" to the tad of my cousin, Bertha.

I was left standing near the front room door; Bertha, one of my cousins and her mam came across to me.

"Bertha," auntie Ruth said, "Say hello to Cousin Anya." Bertha was a stout little girl. She was only six but already had a distinct attitude. Her nose was upturned, and she always held her head up high as if she was better than everyone else around her.

"Hello, Anya, do you remember me?" Bertha asked.

"Yes, little Bertha," I replied.

"I am *not* little anymore," Bertha exclaimed angrily.

I looked up at auntie Ruth who gave me a look which said, *just go with it.*

"Oh yes, I see, Bertha. You're all grown up now."

Walking to the drawing-room, I spotted Mam-gu smoking a cigarette, a nasty habit she herself confessed she'd picked up in her travels to America. I despised people who smoked but not Mam-gu as her kind heart more than made up for it.

"Anya, come sit," she said, patting the seat next to her. I could tell she was worried.

Mam-gu's drawing-room was huge. There were two leather couches at opposite ends of the room and a large coffee table. At one end, a warm, inviting hearth blazed and next to it stood a very grand bookshelf. Above the hearth, hung an impressive photo of Tad-cu. I didn't remember him. He had passed away before I was two. Mam-gu was yet to recover. I sat next to Mam-gu gingerly. I knew she had bad hips.

"So, how's life treating you then, my dear?" she asked, taking another puff of her cigarette making me cough slightly.

"Alright, I guess," I responded. "I'm a bit worried about Mam though."

"What in the world's wrong with her?" Her voice was full of worry.

"It's just that she has been ill a *lot* lately."

"Oh, Anya. It's that time of the year where everyone's getting the flu. Your mam will be fine. In fact, she seemed fine to me the last two times she stopped by here. Give her my love when you get back. Tell her, I'll be round to see her tomorrow.

Relieved, I said, "Thanks, Mam-gu, I was getting anxious."

"Oh, Anya. Say hello to Cousin Alfred." Mam-gu beckoned Alfred over to her. He was my oldest cousin.

"Anya, hello." He smirked at me. I hadn't seen him for ages and he looked so much older. Mam had told me Alfred was now a police officer.

"Hello, Alfred," I grumbled.

"Nice to see you too!" He laughed then returned to partying. Alfred was one of my most hated cousins. I never forgot the way he used to torment me so when I was much younger. The rest of evening went by surprisingly rapidly. I found Annabel and Jemima whose first Holy Communion it was. I congratulated her and made a bit of small talk. They were Bertha's older sisters. It figured I thought to myself. It was easy to tell where Bertha got her attitude from. My favourite cousin Rose wasn't there. I missed her dearly. My Uncle Alexander, Mam's older brother had got himself a fine job in Bangor and they'd all moved there. I didn't interact much with my cousins much to Mam-gu's chagrin.

She let me read one of her books — *Pride and Prejudice* by Jane Austen. Just as I was getting to a *good* bit, we were called into the dining room. Time to eat.

Dinner looked very grand. A large variety of food was laid along the dining table. Salted pork with corn, carrots, leek, roast beef sprinkled with herbs, and cakes and sweets of many flavours which adorned the sideboard for dessert.

I caught Tad's eye and he gave me a look which said, "mind your manners."

Mam always warned me not to consume too much at events, but I sometimes couldn't help myself. Today was none of those days. I ended up eating royally.

Not long after, Tad wanted us to head back. He didn't like to leave Mam alone for too long. Mam-gu saw us out.

"Good-bye, Anya," she said, kissing my cheek. Mam-gu nodded at Tad.

As we walked out, she called, "Greet your mam for me, dearie. Tell her I'll be round tomorrow."

It was getting dark outside, and, thinking about the notorious gangster Tad had described, I gripped onto Tad's arm tightly until we got in safely through our front door. Mam looked pretty much the same but at least she was sat up in bed reading.

The next morning, I was up early for some painting. I heard Tad leave early for his hour-long Sunday walk during which he read the paper. I attempted painting myself with no such luck as my face ended up lopsided. After a while, I called for Mam to come and see what she thought of my efforts.

"Mam."

No answer.

"Mam?"

Still no answer. I thought she may be asleep so I opened the door to her room and gasped. She was lying on the floor — unconscious.

Seven

Life Changer

I bawled over her limp body until Tad got back.
"Anya? Maria?" he said.

"Tad!" I wept.

Hearing my crying, he walked in and froze, standing as still as a statue.

"Wh — what happened..."

He fell to his knees, his eyes glassy.

"Anya, run to the hospital. Now!"

I rushed down the stairs tripping over my own legs. My eyesight was so blurry from crying. I couldn't even breathe properly. My lungs felt like they had turned to stone.

I fumbled for my shoes and coat then dashed out the door. The wind was blowing my hair into my face making it even more difficult to see where I was going. I was running faster than I ever had in my entire twelve years of life but when I got to the hospital, I was apprehensive about going inside. The only time I had been to the hospital was for check-ups twice a year, but I'd always gone with Mam or sometimes Tad. Now, the hospital looked much vaster and much more intimidating. Its walls were rough stone which was rugged to the touch. There was a big banner up on the front of the building which read, 'Caerdydd Ysbyty' (Cardiff Hospital). I was hesitant, yes, but my mam had her very existence hanging in the balance and every second I spent wavering, not sure to go in or not, she could be losing more and more life. I couldn't think about it, I just had to go inside.

Two rows of benches lined the right side of the room crowded with people who looked unwell in one way or the other. Sat at a desk, next to the benches in the waiting room was an older gentleman. He wore rimless glasses which made him look like a professor. His nose was small and scrunched up. Maybe because of all his sniffing and sneezing.

"ATTCHOOO! Yes, how may I help you? Wait one moment — it's coming—TAKE COV...AAATTCHOOOO!" The doctor (I could tell by squinting at his name tag. It read Dr Sneelp) desperately tried to cover his nose, but huge chunks of snot and mucus flew out of his nose like flying saucers, covering some unlucky patients nearby. Fortunately for me, I was agile so I dodged out of the way of the flying catarrh but the rest of the patients, who were mostly dear old ladies, found it harder to dart away. If they weren't sick before they definitely were now.

Before long, most of the queue dispersed so I quickly jumped up to Dr Sneelp's desk. He sniffled a bit and blew into his tissue before saying,

"Hello, young lady. Can I help you?"

"Yes, hello. My mam...sh — she's unconscious. Hurry!"

"My, my! Well — I should have to get the boys out? Hmm..."

"Quickly!" I was moving and hopping from leg to leg as I would do if I needed to use the lavatory.

"One minute, please. What's your address missy? "82 Coveny Road, just before you turn right onto Walker Road," I told him.

"Hmm — the team should do it! I go and fetch them now. You sit there and wait for me," Dr Sneelp instructed.

I sat down on one of the benches. It was very uncomfortable and I kept shifting to try and get the right position. I decided I wasn't going to listen to silly old Dr Sneelp. I was going back home to my mam whether he liked it or not. I got up and ran home.

I sprinted upstairs to check on Mam. She was still lying on the floor, eyes closed, lips pressed tightly shut.

I didn't like to see Mam like this at all so I went downstairs and kept a watch through the parlour window for the hospital staff.

The hospital carriage arrived in what seemed like hours. I shouted for Tad to come. He rushed to the door immediately.

Strange men in white cloaks came into the house carrying a stretcher and even stranger medical equipment. They moved swiftly as their alert eyes scanned around, looking for the patient. The men walked upstairs into Mam's and Tad's bedroom. They picked her up, placed her on the stretcher and gingerly carried her back to their carriage. I pushed my way forward hoping to go with Mam to the hospital.

One of the men turned to me. "We're very sorry but you cannot accompany her."

"I must go, Anya," Tad said, softly. "It'll be alright. She will be fine. You take word to your mam-gu as she might be on her way here. Then come back home to wait for me."

I wailed and cried — I had to be with her — but the men ignored me like I was a fly, and whisked my Mam away.

I shook violently as I walked back into the house. Cradling myself on the couch I cried and cried. Life was perfect. I'd have a delicious breakfast every morning, Mam and I would walk peacefully to school. Tad would come in and sometimes bring me chocolates. I cried even more. Just the thought of her in a stiff, hospital bed like the ones I'd seen in books upset me. By this time, my nose was running and my eyes were so sore they felt itchy. Making my way to Mam-gu was hard. My legs didn't want to move. I had a pain lodged in my chest. My thoughts raced with all the 'what ifs?'

Mam-gu took one look at my tear-soaked face and knew something wasn't right. She held my hand and led me in.

"What happened Anya?" she asked almost shrieking.

"It's Mam," I wailed, and burst into tears.

"Shhhh child," she said hugging me. "What happened?"

"I found her lying on the floor unconscious and now Tad and the hospital men have taken her to the hospital.

At that, Mam-gu fled to the cloakroom for a shawl and some shoes.

"Have you eaten?"

"No Mam-gu but I am not hungry."

"No no you must eat, I'll get you some sandwiches. When you're done, see yourself out and go home. I'll head to the hospital."

When I got home, I was so exhausted, I passed out. I dreamt of Mam, alone, in a ward, coughing feverishly with her skin so pale it was almost green. Her hair was pulled pack with a ribbon I had given her and her lips were invisible to the naked eye.

I woke up with a start and chided myself for being so foolish. She would get through this, a little unconsciousness did not mean she was close to death. Surely?

I heard Tad slip back into the house later that evening. I ran downstairs to meet him.

"I cannot stay with your mam," his voice caught in his throat. "No visitor is allowed to stay the night at the hospital. "Your mam-gu is still there but should be leaving shortly." His eyes were red and he avoided my gaze.

I was dying to ask how Mam was but from how Tad looked, I wasn't sure I wanted to hear the answer.

"Let us go to bed now, Anya."

I couldn't bear to sleep alone so I cuddled up to Tad in their bed.

* * *

At the crack of dawn, someone rapped on the door. Tad walked down the wooden stairs, me behind him. With every knock I heard, my heart thudded. I reminded myself to breathe as Tad peeked through the creaky, oak door. Two men in black stood there when Tad opened the door. They took off their hats.

"We are so very sorry. Your wife didn't make it. She passed away a little while ago."

I looked up at them — it must be a trick — but their cold eyes and sombre looks told me this was very, very real.

"Tad!" I choked, my voice shaking. I felt like throwing up. I felt like smashing something. To be honest, I felt like kicking the men in black *and* the hospital men. Tad hugged me fiercely, crying into my shaggy hair whilst I bawled into his nightshirt.

Finally, with near-crimson eyes, Tad turned to the men and said to them, "Thank you."

Thank you? Thank you for telling me the only one who understood and was kind to me (apart from Tad) was gone!

One of the men grunted, "We'll come back in a couple of days to discuss the funeral arrangements. Good day."

"Good day?" I shouted. "It's a horrific day!" But they had already gone. We stayed at home all day, mostly in silence. Neither Tad or I had any inclination to eat.

Eventually, Tad said, "Well I'm going to go and let your mam-gu and work know what has happened."

He choked as he said the last word.

I nodded solemnly.

"You should come and stay at your mam-gu's while I take the message to work as I shan't be going for some days."

The thought of seeing Mam-gu as she took the news filled me more dread.

"No Tad. I'll stay upstairs."

Tad was taking hours and hours, so after a while, I decided to get some fresh air. The first people I saw were old Mo and Pat.

"Hello, Anya!"

Bad news does travel fast.

"We are so sorry about your mam. How's your Tad?" Pat lowered her head.

"He's bearing up. He had to go to his work and to my Mam-gu's," I said and I carried on walking, not wanting to stop and chat.

"Alright dear, bye now!" Mo said.

I walked along the cobblestone road, keeping my head down in case I bumped into somebody else I knew. I vaguely listened to the birds tweeting in the distance and men shouting down the road in Splott market. I could see young orphans performing wildly on the streets, their hats laid out for pennies.

I kept on walking not sure where I was going. Before long I found myself in a long alleyway which smelt like rotting cabbage soup. The dark walls felt wet to the touch and there was garbage covering the gravelly ground.

A black cat with yellow eyes emerged from the rubbish bags and stared intently at me, hissing and spitting.

"Good kitty — good kitty. Ow!" I cried as the cat leapt up on me before dashing away. I looked down at my knees. Luckily, there were only minor scratches there, but it still stung like spraying perfume on an open wound.

I should've gone with the cat.

Two young boys, around my age, stomped into the alleyway. Even though they were around my height, their build was bullish and they looked rock hard.

They cornered me, staring me straight in the eye.

"What shall we do with this one eh, George?"

"Let's take her money and teach her a lesson for being in our alleyway!"

They cackled like villains as they advanced towards me.

"Please!" I cried, "I don't have any money just leave me alone!"

"No," George said. "Not a chance."

"My mam is dead!" I begged.

"She just died and I..."

"Save it." The other boy said.

"Yeah. All my family's dead and I ain't whinging, am I?" George stated.

"I know what you feel like! It's difficult I know that" I cried. For a fleeting instant, George got a longing look in his eyes and I thought I'd succeeded but then he refocused on me.

"No! They left me! Now you're going to get hurt!"

"Wh — what did I do?" I stammered.

George ran at me and punched me in the nose before I had time to dodge. Blood trickled down my dress staining the cotton. The other boy kicked my shin and I screamed. I tried to get up but all the pain made it very difficult to move anywhere. Then, a distant, tiny whistle blew. It got closer and closer and the two boys halted.

"Oh shoot!" The second boy cursed. "The police."

George glared at me once more, threw a banana peel at my face and sprinted back down the alleyway. I lay there shuddering and frozen in shock at the atrocious events of the day. Could it get any worse? The policeman came into the dark alleyway and ran over to me.

"Are you alright, miss?" he asked.

His voice sounded familiar. I studied him, still dazed by what I'd just been through.

It was dark but I could make out he was tall and muscular with a shaved beard and bushy eyebrows with a wart on his left cheek. It was Alfred, my cousin.

"Anya?" Alfred queried, "Is that you?"

"Yes," I said obviously, "Now could you help me up?" Alfred lifted me and brushed the rubbish off me.

"Your nose — and how are you here? I just heard the news about your mam."

"I walked, obviously!" I said disdainfully.

"My nose was punched and you took so long with your whistle you couldn't even catch the thugs."

"So sorry to hear about your mam, but you shouldn't be out by yourself on a day like this least of all in a place like this."

"Could you describe these thugs for me, please?"

"My height, both with black hair and built like bulls," I recited. "Got it?"

"Thank you."

We stood in tense silence for a couple of minutes then he said. "I'm dreadfully sorry about Aunt Maria."

"Well sorry isn't going to bring her back is it!"

"Anya, I'm only trying to help! Why are you always so difficult?" Alfred declared.

"Well, I don't need your blimmin' help!" I shouted.

I ran off covering my bloody nose as I dodged carriages, cats and dogs. I pounded heavily on the door once I got home.

Tad opened it and I momentarily forgot about my injury. "Anya!" He exclaimed. "My god — where have you been? What happened?..."

I told him reluctantly about the bullies and my awkward encounter with cousin Alfred, not wanting to give him any more grief.

After he cleaned me up, we sat down on the sofa in silence hugging each other. I thought about Mam and how I missed her so much.

"It's getting late, time to rest, Anya."

I didn't need persuading. I crashed onto my bed, plunging into horrific nightmares. It started with the screaming. All I could hear was screaming and all I could see was pitch-black darkness. Then, Mam appeared, lying motionless in her hospital bed whilst doctors flapped about like swans around her. I could not move. My body was frozen so all I could do was observe this horrible scene. More doctors came through a door holding a large black coffin. They picked Mam up and laid her gently inside it. I tried to break free and shout but I was stone stiff.

"Anya!" A voice called.

Was it Mam?

"Anya!" It called again. "Wake up!"

I felt myself being shaken from side to side.

"ANYA!"

Opening my eyes, I woke up to see Tad's worried face leaning over me.

Eight

The Funeral

*I*wanted time to keep still but it just wouldn't. The dreaded day had come. The days in between had been a flurry of picking out flowers, choosing what clothes to put Mam in, writing a poem for Mam and too many people calling. For most days during that period, I couldn't bear the thought of going to school. So I stayed home with Tad and moped. Mam-gu and my Mam's family came to visit. Mam-gu was distraught. She helped pack Mam's things away, giving me some of Mam's trinkets and the box of letters Mam had written but not given me. Tad didn't have many relatives. He had been an only child too and both his parents were long gone. It had been days since we found Mam — dead. But it all felt like minutes ago.

On that day, I woke up unnaturally early and lay in bed for about an hour thinking and thinking about what could happen that day. Tad knocked on my door

"Come in," I sighed, sitting up.

"Good morning, my lovely," Tad said. He came in and sat down on my bed.

"I know it's hard my love. It is for me too. Extremely so. But we must stick together and hopefully, we shall weather this storm."

I wished there was something I could do to make it all go away.

"Get ready now, we have a long day ahead of us."

Tad's eyes were swollen and red, but he managed to put up a stoic front. He went downstairs to make a quick breakfast whilst I washed my face and body in the bathroom. I couldn't stop thinking about Mam. This was not happening. It hardly felt real. It had all happened so suddenly.

After I'd eventually washed, I searched through my closet for anything black. I managed to find a jet-black dress and a navy overcoat which I wore with some navy stockings.

Breakfast was sugared milk and a cheese sandwich that tasted like sand. I ate mindlessly enough to give me a horrible case of the hiccups. Luckily, with the help of a fresh glass of water, they went away.

Immediately after breakfast, the black carriage bearing Mam arrived. Leaning against Mam's casket was a wreath which read, "Mam." It was full of daisies, Mam's favourite flower. We sat behind the carriage man and as we rode, I viewed the Cardiff sights from the window.

The market was on again — dogs and cats roamed the streets in search of scraps of meat and bones and men and women fought stridently for customers to come to their stalls. They seemed not to have a care in the world. As we approached the church, I spotted my cousins, aunties and uncles waiting outside, all carrying flowers. Through work, Tad had managed to get Mam's funeral and burial arranged at the Anglican Church of St. Mary the Virgin, on Bute Street. It had been built by the Second Marquess of Bute, the same Marquess who built the docks Tad worked at.

They formed an orderly queue and followed us inside as Tad and I walked behind the pallbearers. Mo and Pat were sat at the back of the church. There were long wooden pews of conjoined chairs like a park bench. Tad and I sat on the front row whilst the pallbearers rested Mam at the front of the church. I saw Mam-gu, sitting in the pew to the right of us, sobbing into her kerchief. Aunt Ruth was sat next to her, rubbing her shoulder. I badly wanted to have a look at Mam but Tad said it would be distressing. I strongly disagreed but wasn't in the frame of mind to argue with Tad on such a day.

Apart from family functions which involved a church service, I'd hardly been to church. I looked up at the colourful windows letting in streaks of rainbow light. The windows had pictures on them, like the collages we did at school.

The priest began the service. He was short and quite old with a strange looking triangle hat. His hair was in little tufts which stuck out around the rim of his hat. He wore a long white robe with buttons on the front.

The priest then sang and almost everyone joined in without the need of hymnals, apart from Tad and I who were not church-goers; we sang along from the hymn book. After the hymn, the old priest read from what must have been the bible — I think. I was lost in thought and only returned to the present when Tad got up from his seat next to me to address the sympathisers.

"Good morning everybody," he stated, "Today is a dreadful day. Even so, I know Maria, my wife, is now at peace compared to her life of the last few months as her health was failing, and she'll be much more peaceful than in dreary Cardiff."

There was some low murmuring. Tad waited for the noise to stop then he continued.

"Anya and I miss her so much already. Words cannot describe how much," Tad's voice caught and he let a tear trickle down his cheek before saying, "Maria had a beautiful laugh and smile, a kind, forgiving heart and was always so generous. We are not sure what the future holds for our family without Maria but I have a young daughter who needs me so in that I must find strength. I would like us all, today, to remember my beautiful wife and Anya's caring mam. Those are the memories she would have wanted us to keep. Thank you."

Some just nodded, some cried as Tad quickly wiped his eyes and sat back down next to me. Mamgu went up to say something but it was too much for her. Auntie Ruth led her back to her seat. I understood. At the last minute, I had decided to save the poem I had written for Mam with the letters she had written to me over the years. I couldn't do it.

We all sang a couple more hymns then the service was over. Everyone went outside for Mam's burial. Standing next to Tad, we held each other closely and sobbed together. As Mam's body was lowered into the grave, I turned away. I knew she was gone but seeing it made it ten times worse. People placed flowers around Mam's coffin and some bent down on their knees and prayed.

* * *

At the reception, there were funeral biscuits made of molasses, caraway seeds and ginger. I had no interest in these or the jam, ham and cheese sandwiches. Most people seemed to forget all about the service in a matter of minutes and started talking about babies and other ridiculous things. I was *furious*! How could they have already forgotten about my mam's funeral so quickly?

I went outside and found Tad kneeling alone beside Mam's grave. His eyes were closed and his hands were tenderly placed on the soft earth.

"Tad?"

He turned to me, his eyes puffy.

"Hello, my dear. What is it?" I told him how everyone had already moved on but he just laughed lightly.

"That's what people are like these days," Tad told me. "Some remember, some forget. Quickly."

Stomping my foot in outrage I declared, "Well they should all remember!"

Tad stood up and stroked my hair fondly.

"Go and meet your cousins. I'll be right inside in a minute." I wanted to stay with him but I knew it was difficult enough for him as it was so I obeyed and walked inside.

My cousins Annabel and Jemima were stood awkwardly next to the water table, chatting and twirling their hair.

"Hello, Annabel. Hello Jemima!" I forced a smile, baring all of my teeth. "How are you both?"

"Good, thank you," Annabel said awkwardly.

"We are really sorry about your mam, Anya," Jemima offered uncomfortably. They couldn't look me in the eye like my Mam dying was some crime.

"Thank you," I said softly, shifting from foot to foot. "I am going to go and sit down."

"Bye, Anya," Annabel said.

Mam-gu was sat in a corner, being comforted by a group of women.

I wandered over to an isolated bench and sat down. I thought about Mam — how she loved singing. How she reassured me when I was worried. I even remembered little things like her favourite colour being navy. I could hear her captivating laughter. It sounded so clear it was as though she was standing right next to me.

When everyone had gone, Tad and I headed home. Finally, the funeral was over but the worst was yet to come.

Nine

Stick Together?

As soon as we got back home, I took to my bed, exhausted. I couldn't believe how tired I was. I curled up in a tiny ball and fell into a deep sleep.

In the morning, I arose into a sea of light. The bright sun was shining through my curtains as I got up. It must be nearly midday. The sun was quite strong.

Without washing myself or brushing my teeth, I dragged my body downstairs. Tad was sitting on the sofa in the parlour, staring into space. I sat next to him and leant on his shoulder.

"How are you my dear," he said, stroking my head.

I didn't reply. I think he knew how I was feeling.

The next few weeks and months went by in a blur. Tad cried a lot. I cried a lot. It wasn't easy being without a mother . Not a moment went by without me thinking of Mam. I returned to school, most days walking myself as Tad had to work more hours at the docks now that we no longer had the extra money Mam used to bring in from her job at the sewing cottage. Tad often left for work at the crack of dawn and stayed to work some more hours after I came home from school, although he was usually back home before sundown. He did his best to keep me from being sad but I could see he was struggling so much to deal with Mam's absence himself.

* * *

To drown the sorrows of grief and tiredness, Tad would sometimes stop at the ale house on his way home — one or two days a week for an hour or two. It soon became a habit. Not only that, the more he kept this habit, the fouler his mood got. I found myself treading on eggshells more and more each time Tad came home late. Once or twice, I had ventured out to fetch Tad from the alehouse. It was a huge place filled mostly with drunken, brawling men. I decided not to repeat the trip anymore.

Most days, it was alright. I got used to it. It was the breath that reeked of ale I found hard to deal with. It would follow him everywhere he went in the house until he had a wash. Even then, it was still there. I would make supper and wait until Tad came home for us to eat together.

On one particular Saturday, Tad was especially late. He was usually home to prepare lunch by noon. I got quite worried but with nothing to do other than wait, I flicked through some books while I waited for him to arrive.   Suddenly, I heard a double knock at the front door. It must already be at least four o'clock.

Finally! Tad stood there but he looked — drowsy. More drowsy than usual. His hair was limp — it looked like he had swapped it for damp straw — and his clothes were muddy and slightly ripped. His eyes were sagging and he was swaying from side to side.

"Oh, Tad..."

I helped him inside and onto the couch in the living room intending to talk to him but he dozed off as soon as his head hit the cushion. I sat opposite him on the single couch. I wondered what would become of us if Tad carried on like this. He couldn't cope with the fact that Mam had passed away so he was drinking to resolve it. Instead of us sticking together as he promised, he was confiding in ale and beer. It seemed Mam had been the only reliable part of this family and now it was like a triangle losing one of its corners — it just wasn't whole anymore. I was angry but I couldn't bring myself to take it out on Tad. We both had been through too much these last few months.

When Tad eventually woke up an hour or so later, he was in the worst mood.

"Anya! Don't just sit there gawping, get me a sandwich or something!"

I was shocked and, to be honest, a little bit scared. Tad had hardly ever spoken to me like that before. Hurriedly, I prepared a jam sandwich and gave it to him. He ate it greedily making me realise how hungry I was so, I made one for myself too. In my worry, I hadn't eaten. I ate in an uncomfortable silence and gradually plucked up the courage to talk to him.

"Where were you, Tad?"

"I was with a couple of friends, Anya."

"But where?"

"Anya, it's none of your business now go to your room!"

I ran upstairs crying. I wondered, what sort of man had my Tad become? I ached for Mam so badly. It was like the way you ache for food if you're famished, but ten times worse.

Needing some fresh air, I crept downstairs dodging any creaky steps I could remember and opened the front door.

"Anya?" Tad called from the parlour.

Great, here we go.

"You stay in this house you hear m…"

The last thing I wanted to do was listen to him, so for the first time ever, I disobeyed. Okay, maybe not the first time, but the first time in a long while. I ran aimlessly through the dark streets without an idea of where I was going.

And then I suddenly knew. I was going to Mam-gu's house. Mam-gu always knew how to cheer me up. It was either a nice warm cup of tea or a hug — either worked just as well.

I knocked three times — a knocking ritual mam-gu and I both followed — so she knew it was me. Her kind withered faced peered out of the door to greet me.

"Anya! So good to see you, my darling girl! What are you doing here so late? Come in for heaven's sake or you'll catch a cold if not your death out there!"

She led me into her cosy living room. Mam-gu hugged me. A little too tightly.

"I. Can't. Breathe!" I gasped for air as I pushed away.

"Sorry, Anya. I don't know my own strength!" She chuckled. We sat down and I wrapped myself with a worn-out but comfortable blanket.

The warm welcoming hearth crackled as I sank into my chair. I felt safe here and I never wanted to leave.

"I'll make us some tea," announced Mam-gu, leaving the room.

I got up and walked around the room with a little dance in between. I glided my fingers across the rough book covers and imagined my finger was a paintbrush. I 'painted' along the china set Mam-gu had put out neatly on her small table and across the embroidery on her soft pillows.

"Lovely waltzing my dear!" Mam-gu exclaimed, holding a tray with two steaming mugs of tea on them, "I used to be quite the dancer myself back in the day."

I quickly stopped, embarrassed, and sat down.

Mam-gu passed me a cup.

"Ow!" I yelped, dropping it. "That's boiling!"

With amazing speed, Mam-gu caught the falling mug without spilling anything!

"Bravo!" I clapped.

She stood up and bowed whilst I laughed at how deft she was.

"I'm just happy my knees are holding together," she said. "Last night, they were really playing up!"

We sat in silence for a while.

Mam-gu said, "Anya, you don't pop by as much as I'd like you to so what's the occasion?" I sat in silence again for a bit.

"Tad, Mam-gu. He's changed. He's become quite harsh with me."

Mam-gu stared into empty space for a while before reaching over to hug me. She winced, clutching her back.

"Good Lord — I am so sorry Anya."

Mam-gu looked upset but not too much like she already knew it was coming. I told her the rest through small sips of tea: how Tad had started drinking, gambling, occasionally struggling to keep up with the heating bills and how I felt lost and alone now.

"Listen, Anya. You know I'm always here. Like me and your mam, you are a strong young woman and I know you can get through this. Bad things happen so good can break through." I didn't understand what she was saying, but I knew she meant well, and I thanked her for that.

"Mam-gu?" I asked.

"Yes, Anya?"

"Could I possibly, um, stay with you?" I did my best puppy dog eyes. "I feel I have no home now. I'm so lost and desperate!"

"Oh, my love! Your tad may be drinking but he's still your tad. Besides, he'd have the police on me for 'kidnapping' you!"

I sighed.

"Maybe you should be heading back, dear," Mam-gu said, "It's getting awfully late."

"Yes. Thank you so much, Mam-gu."

I hugged her, left her living-room and then out through the front door.

There was a strong wind outside, blowing my hair into my face. My dress was rising higher than I'd have liked it to, so I had to hold it down whilst walking *and* spitting hair out of my mouth.

With a sigh of relief that the treacherous journey home was over, I banged on the door. Tad came out and looked me up down before letting me in. His face was expressionless. I quickly shut the door behind me, so as not to let any wind in. I went to make myself hot cocoa after taking my shoes off at the front door. To get onto Tad's good side, I made him one too, placing them both onto a metal tray. Carrying the drinks into the living room, I placed them on the small table.

"Light the fire will you," Tad called from the kitchen.

Why was he so calm? I wondered.

I gathered logs from the pile in the corner of the room and threw them into the empty firebox. Fire danced before my eyes and lit up my face. How I wished we could go back to the way things were.

Turning around, I noticed some furniture wasn't there. The second sofa had disappeared and so had the cabinet which stood in the corner of the parlour.

"What happened to all the furniture?" I questioned as Tad walked in.

"Where were you, Anya?" Tad asked, sipping his drink and ignoring my question.

No thank you from him or anything but I didn't mention that. "I was at..." I was apprehensive to tell him I was at Mam-gu's.

"Spit it out!" He ordered.

"Mam-gu's," I said. "I was at Mam-gu's for a little bit."

"A little bit! You were gone for two hours. What were you doing with that old hag?"

"She is not a hag!" I cried, defensively.

"She is loving and kind and doesn't drink so much she can't even walk!"

I covered my mouth quickly in case anything else came out of it. Why, oh why had I said that. To my great surprise and luck for that matter, Tad just stared at me. For a moment, he looked like he was going to cry.

He carried on staring and I didn't want to find out what would come at the end of it, so I got up silently, picked up my still-full mug of cocoa and escaped upstairs. Who knew what tomorrow would bring?

Ten

It's All Downhill From Here

*T*he last six months had been horrible. My Saturday morning visits to Mam-gu were the only ray of sunshine. Tad had now started drinking almost every night and often came back late or the next morning leaving me an ambiguous note when it took his fancy. He would always shout and order me around mercilessly however hard I tried to put him in good moods. The house was nearly bare because of his gambling. Most of the furniture had been taken away to recover Tad's gambling debts and soon enough, the house itself would be gone as well. We couldn't afford to pay for hot water most months and before long we moved the basin outside to use the makeshift water heater Tad's ale house friend had designed. Food was scarce as we barely had any money and sometimes had to make do with scraps. 'Saving food' Tad called it, but I called it 'poverty.'

My school had become an occasional relief because it wasn't often Tad could afford the school pence. When I did go, I found most of the children avoided me like the plague. I often wondered if losing one's Mam was contagious. On this particular day, I was glad to be going. Outside, I scrubbed myself hard in the washbasin with carbolic soap which stung my eyes. I hoped, if I scrubbed hard enough, I would remove from me all the bad things that had happened recently. Wishful thinking was what it was. When I'd dressed for school, I brushed my teeth and went down for breakfast, whatever that was these days. There was another note from Tad which I didn't even bother to read. I knew what it would say. I sat down eating as I pondered. What could I do? I wasn't needed or wanted here.

* * *

My thirteenth birthday came and went; Mam-gu got me something worthwhile. A new dress and some boots, which I saved for special occasions. Tad got some trinkets from the market. I was happy at least he remembered. One Saturday in the following spring, Gwenllian, Old Mo's daughter stopped by for a visit. She was back in Cardiff visiting her family and had heard about Mam. She'd since moved on from the workhouses to London where she got herself a job as a maid in one of the grand houses there. She looked all grown up, well-fed and happy. Gwenllian had always been nice to me. I had a lovely afternoon listening to her tales of London and all the things they got up to there. This was one of the rare days Tad made it home early, somewhat sober. Payday was a way off yet. It was usual. There was a pattern. He seemed a bit more like his usual self for the last week or so before payday. So he sat with Gwenllian and me, taking a keen interest in her stories.

On Sunday, I heard Tad leave early. For a short time, it was as if everything was back to normal. Tad, going out for his Sunday walk to grab the Gazette, Mam waking up and cooking up a storm. I sat up to look at my school books. It was the only way I could manage not be too many miles behind. Not that it helped with things like Arithmetic. I pulled the box from underneath my bed. It was next to the box with Mam's letters. I stared at the box for a moment, my eyes welling up. Some days, when I could handle it, I would sit and read the letters many times over. They made me feel like Mam was near. On other days, like today, I somehow couldn't bear the thought.

Tad returned a little while later. I heard the door slam shut. He was rambling on. I caught bits and pieces of what he was saying when he spoke louder.

"Romeo, oh, Romeo..."

"Fair is foul, and foul is fair."

"Hover through the fog and filthy air."

It finally clicked.

"Shakespeare?" I said disdainfully.

Tad had been known to break out into one of these recitals whenever he was happy. Was there anything to be happy about these days.

I thought to myself that maybe the alcohol had affected him in some strange way.

Traipsing downstairs, I saw Tad reading the Gazette in the parlour.

I headed for the kitchen to make the last scraps of pork, some potatoes and carrots for lunch. After what turned out to be not such a bad lunch, Tad headed back to the parlour whilst I cleaned up.

"Anya," he called out. As I stepped into the parlour, he looked up, smiled and beckoned me over. He actually smiled.

"Look here Anya," he said tapping a page on the paper. I peered over his shoulder to see that he was pointing at a job advertisement.

Confused, I looked at Tad. If we couldn't afford to live in Cardiff, how could we live in London with all the things I'd heard from Gwenllian about how expensive it was.

"You want to take a job in London Tad?"

"Oh, no — this is for you. You see Gwenllian got me thinking. So I looked in the Gazette and as luck would have it, there a maid's job open and it starts in two weeks."

"I shall head into Queen Street and telephone the number tomorrow."

I looked at Tad in complete shock.

"But I don't want to go to London!"

"Who will look after you, Tad?"

"I don't need looking after Anya and besides, it'll be for your own good to get a job."
I spun on my heels.

"Where are *you* going then?" Tad asked as I made my way to the stairs.

"To my room," I murmured.

"Excuse me? Speak up girl!" he shouted.

"To my room!" I shouted back and I ran upstairs.

I threw myself onto my bed and sobbed myself silly. I couldn't sleep despite many attempts to do so, so I decided to get a book off the shelf to read. I waited for a while then got out of my bed and when I did — *'CREEK!'*

The floorboards groaned under me as I stepped off the bed. I waited five seconds, just in case Tad had heard me, but all I could hear was him reciting

Shakespeare monotonously downstairs. I sighed in relief and reached for my art box. Somehow, I'd managed to keep my supplies. My brush glided across the canvas. Hues of blues, yellows and greens danced about, merged and blended. I painted the sky a brilliant azure colour and the grass different shades of green.

Gradually, after nearly an hour of painting, my eyes began to droop, and I set my brushes and paint pot down on the floor and went to sleep on my stiff, wooden bed.

Tad did telephone the job advertisers the next day, as promised. I peeped at the advertisement when he was having a wash. It said 'Scullery Maid' wanted at Tippets House. What exactly was a scullery maid? I really didn't want to find out. However grand Gwenllian had made London sound, I didn't want to leave Tad, or Mam-gu or Cardiff.

Tad came back looking relieved, but with a hint of sadness about him. I felt sorry for him. He informed me that I had been awarded the job and would be on a train to London in two weeks. I begged, cried and tried to cajole Tad out of it but his mind was set. I even tried to enlist Mam-gu's help, which proved unsuccessful; the relationship she had with Tad had gone from bad to non-existent since Mam had died.

Alas, it was my fate. I was to go to London. The fourteen days in between flew past. I cried and cried and cried as I bid Mam-gu farewell. Our days at home were mostly spent in silence but even on my last day 'he' was out at it again until late.

Eleven

London

"Wake up Anya! Wake up!" Tad shouted, exasperatedly

Rubbing my tired eyes, I squinted up at him.

"Come on! You need to be off! It's your first day and you want to be late?"

"Late for what?" I asked sleepily.

Then it dawned on me. Today was the day. I was off to London. To be a maid. A tidal wave of dread came over me — much like killer bees.

"Tad? Do I have to go? Please don't make me go!" I started to cry.

"'Course you do, Anya! Do I look like a wealthy man to you? Now stop blubbering like a baby and get ready!"

He had a point about not looking like a wealthy man though. His shirt was tattered, and his eyes were bloodshot from drinking too much ale. Hesitantly, I walked outside to the washtub as everything in the bathroom was gone.

Great, I thought as I turned on the pump, *no warm water.* At least I was used to it — we hardly ever had warm water anymore. The bath did help though. The bitter cold made me awake and alert, ready for anything which came my way. I trudged back into the house, pulling my boots along, then I found a note on the table.

To Anya,
  Your suitcase is packed, and your train ticket is under the doormat. Do something good with your life and earn some money.

How had Tad written that and left so quickly? I pulled on my leather boots, picked up my case and took my train ticket from under the doormat. I was to catch the 10:48 train. Walking to the train station, I saw Old Mo and Pat knitting on their doorstep.

"Morning!" I called to them.
One might say 'good morning' but this morning was not one of the good kinds.

"Good morning, Anya!" They called together.

* * *

At the station platform, I was suddenly startled by the shrill whistle of the awaiting train. I looked up at the strangely fascinating vehicle. Its many large wheels were all connected to a long body. I had never been on a train before. There were many carriages attached to the engine by enormous hooks, and a tall funnel was spewing smoke. I stood there awestruck by the marvel until a guard blew a whistle twice and shouted "All aboard, all aboard." The 10:48 train for London was about to leave!

"Wait! Wait!" I called as the train started to move forward slowly, with jets of steam blowing across the platform.

"Ticket, please," said the uniformed station worker as I ran to the nearest carriage.

"Here!" I thrust my ticket into his palm and leapt onto the train.

"'Scuse me miss," I said.

"Sorry, sir," I apologised.

"I beg your pardon madam."

Bumping into adults and children alike, I finally found a seat and sat down next to an old man who was awfully wheezy.

"Would you like a peppermint?" He asked after a series of coughs into his handkerchief, handing me what looked like a stone.

"No thank you, sir," I replied.

"Oh, I insist!" he offered, smiling.

"No, no! It's fine" I said.

124

"You must have it!"

"Sorry sir, I need to go to the WC," I said, crossing my fingers behind my back.

"I'll wait outside for you," the man said most vexingly.

"You don't need to!" I said getting slightly *agitated*.

On returning to my seat, I shuffled as far away from the wheezing man as I could. Luckily, he fell asleep just as the train started rocking and picking up speed. I pressed my face onto the cool glass window. Outside, trees, hills and sheep went swiftly past. Or was it the train? I wasn't quite sure. There were rows of little white cottages with thatched roofs and honeysuckle growing out of them. Green fields filled with grazing sheep and adorable lambs. After a while, the train drew to a stop. Gloucester, the sign said.

"Everybody for Gloucester, off!" the ticket man instructed, strutting down the train aisle like he owned the world.

There was a great faff as men, women and children bustled out of the train. So much so my case was knocked over and was nearly carried away in the stampede.

Luckily, after so many people had left the train, there were a few extra seats, so I moved away from the creepy old man. We set off again. I felt rather hungry, so I rummaged through my case and found a squashed-up sandwich. Most of it was still intact so I crammed it into my mouth and swallowed it with a big gulp.

I fell asleep to the steady chugging of the train and only woke up when it stopped with an almost abrupt halt.

"Last stop. Everyone out!" The ticket man demanded, "We have arrived at Paddington Station."

Pad-ding-ton. Paddington. I liked that word. I wasn't sure of the time so I asked the ticket man the time. It was nearly three! I was supposed to be at Tippets House by three-thirty at the latest! I jumped out of the carriage and looked around. This was nothing like Cardiff! Ladies in strange garments roamed, lugging their exhausted children, and men in suits and ties glanced at their pocket watches.

This will be an adventure!

Paddington was filled to the brim with Londoners. Every turn was like a breath of new, fresh air.

Is it right, or left...?

I decided to ask the friendliest looking person I could find.

"Morning!" I said bobbing my head at him.

"You filthy urchin! Get away from me!" he shouted, giving me a nasty look.

"Oi!" I started to say but he had already turned on his heel and strode into a brisk walk.

Just my luck.

Wanting to stretch the little money I had as much as possible, I decided to hitch a lift. I knew it was dangerous but at that moment I had no other choice. I was tired and starving, so I waved at any vehicles passing by. Finally, one came puffing to a stop.

"Want a ride, young lady?" he asked.

"Oh, yes please, sir!"

He opened the door and I jumped into the strange contraption. It wasn't like anything I'd seen before! It was like a wagon but bigger, with wheels that turned and turned and turned.

"So, young miss, where would you like to go?" the man asked, taking out a tobacco pipe like I'd seen Tad use.

"Tippets House, Kingston Road, please. At least, I think it's Tippets House," I said trying not to choke on the smoke.

"Ah yes. I'm headed that way. Mrs Axton works there. A fine lady she is. Makes nice lamb." I forced a smile.

"Scrawny little thing. How old are ya? Six?" he chuckled at his own joke.

"No, actually! I am nearly thirteen years of age!" I exclaimed with as much dignity as I could muster.

"A baby!" The man stated.

We chugged along in this bizarre thing; my destination trusted in the hands of an odd, ageist stranger.

After what seemed like an eternity, he said "Not long now young lady. Just at the end of this street."

As we neared, I glanced up at the building emerging from all the other houses. My giddy aunt Jemima — the place was huge! I jumped out, thanked the odd man and dashed for the door. I'd had enough of strange men for one day.

I knocked on the door several times until a frustrated looking lady, with a huge bosom, yanked the door open.

"Eh? Who are you?" she asked looking me up and down. "God. Don't tell me *you're* the new maid. Is this their idea of a joke!"

Despite the impolite comments, I smiled and bobbed my head at her.

"Pleased to meet you, ma'am. And yes, as a matter, of fact I am the new maid."

She scowled at me. "You are to call me Mrs Axton."

So, this was the lady the man called fine. She seemed anything but fine to me.

"Well, don't just stand there gawping like a lunatic! Get inside, plenty of work to be done!"

I grabbed my small suitcase and followed Mrs Axton into the house. It was like nothing I'd seen before. In Cardiff, the biggest building I'd seen was the alehouse, where papa spent most of his time, but this was ten times bigger. The floor was covered by a red, wool carpet lined all the way to the stairs. Looking up above, I saw a chandelier, which sparkled in the outside sunlight. We turned and I was led into a kitchen as big as my whole house! Unfortunately, I got little chance to look around as I was forced down into a small room with a mattress on the floor and a mirror on the wall.

"Is this where the other maid sleeps?" I asked.

"No, fool! It is where *you* will be sleeping!" Mrs Axton replied sharply.

I inhaled. "Surely, I should be sleeping somewhere more — inviting," I ventured, fiddling with my hands.

"Insolent child! All skivvies must sleep here for the first couple of years!" Mrs Axton barked.

"Now, I suspect you're hungry."

"Yes, Mrs Axton," I automatically replied.

"Well, I've got some smoked pork done up. You can also meet everyone else here at Tippets House."

I nodded and stared at her.

"Get going then or the meat'll get cold!"

I scurried to the kitchen to find a man and young girl sat at a large wooden table.

As I sat down, the man greeted me saying, "Hello, I am Charles or Charlie if you like. I'm the butler."

"Hello," I responded, "I am Anya, the new housemaid. I don't have another name I'm afraid."

"Oh that is quite alright," Charles reassured, "Anya is a wonderful name in my opinion."

"Thank you," I smiled, "no one has ever said my name is wonderful."

"I am Madeline, but woe betide if you ever call me that," the young girl butted in.

"So, what *should* I call you," I questioned.

"Maud. What else?"

I had already formulated strong opinions of Charles and Maud. Charles was a gentleman and very sweet, whereas Maud was as sour as a lemon drop.

The pork was very enjoyable and as I ate, I told Charles about my life back in Cardiff before Mam died — and all about the journey to Tippets House. He seemed interested and nodded in all the right places. On the other hand, Maud kept picking at her nails, fiddling with her hair and interrupting me with "why" and "when" and "how."'

"Anya. Do not forget to wake up at six-thirty sharp or else Mrs Axton'll skin you alive," Charles whispered.

I thanked him for the advice then went to my room to unpack.

I emptied my small case then opened my box. Inside I kept the letters my mam had written before she passed. I had found them under my pillow.

Holding them tightly to my chest I rocked back and forth. I felt her strong, safe arms around me, telling me everything would be alright. How I longed for her — but all I could do was pretend she was there. I closed my eyes and imagined her protective and loving arms around me...

* * *

I was awoken by the ringing of bells. I rapidly dressed and put on my apron, eager not to be late on my first day. Tucking one of Mam's letters in my pocket, I walked into the kitchen. Unfortunately, my eyes were displeased when I came across Mrs Axton and her huge bosom cooking bacon and eggs.

"Well don't just stand there gawping up at me! Grab some porridge and eat it!"

Yum.

Regardless of the more superior smells coming from the cooker, I relished the sweet porridge and licked my bowl clean.

The first job of the day was to serve the master and mistress breakfast. I was told to carefully carry the food on a tray to their room, knock on the door until I was called in and to place the breakfast on their bedside table.

"No spilling, no dropping, no slipping and no wobbling," Mrs Axton warned.

I walked up the stairs and took a guess at as to which door was the master and mistress's bedroom, and knocked hesitantly, using my foot as my arms were carrying hot, delicious breakfast. It looked delicious in fact I was all but ready to quickly grab a rasher of that crispy bacon when a raspy voice called,

"Come in."

Stepping into the room was like stepping into Wonderland. The room had light straining to be seen through the velvet curtains, a wooden desk with some paper and pens, a king-sized bed adorned with exotic patterns and a fluffy rug on the floor.

"Whoah," I murmured.

"Is that breakfast?" There was that horrible rasp again.

"Uh... yes sir," I bobbed my head.

"Good, very good."

I struggled not to wince at his rasp.

"I see you are new?"

"Yes, sir. My name is Anya and I come from Cardiff. My moth..."

"Too much talking," he interrupted.

"Sorry, sir," I said.

"Mmm..." he mused.

"Marie, dear. Breakfast is here."

"Oh, goodie! Ah, who's this little cutie!"

"I'm Anya, ma'am," I bobbed my head once more.

I cautiously walked backwards, not knowing whether I should stay or leave. I stood still for a while then went out of the room. Inside the hallway, I was met by a young girl.

"Hello. I'm Charity but you can call me... Charity!" She giggled at her attempt at humour.

"How amusing. I am so sorry Miss Charity, also known as Charity, but I must get back to my duties," I said, walking back to the kitchen.

"Duties?" Charity spluttered, "You make it sound so grand. You are the new scullery maid aren't you?"

I kept trying to get used to the ridiculous amount of work I had to do but couldn't and ended up taking a break much to Mrs Axton's displeasure.

"Get up, you lazy child!" Mrs Axton stated, bonking me on the head with a wooden spoon. "Finish those stairs then move straight on to dusting."

"Mae'n gas gen I," I mumbled under my breath.

"You hate it, eh?" Mrs Axton asked, "well, let us see how much you hate havin' no lunch!"

I was stunned that Mrs Axton understood Welsh. I needed to be more careful in my exasperation. I rounded off the stairs and dusting but there were tons of jobs left to be done.

Charles bumped into me in the hallway and seeing my hopeless face said, "don't worry, the first day's always the hardest but it gets much easier."

133

When the time came for dinner I dashed to the kitchen and gobbled up my salted beef ravenously. Excusing myself, I crashed onto my stiff bed and passed out.

* * *

"Argh!" I jumped up as I felt something cold and wet on my face.

"That is what you get for waking up late," Maud grinned, holding a half-full bucket of cold water.

"Did you really have to do that, Maud?" I moaned.

"Just for you, yes!" she exclaimed, "now you had better get up before Mrs Axton comes in. Then there'll be trouble."

For breakfast, I chose to eat porridge once again. It tasted even better than the day before's. Mrs Axton luckily didn't give me any chores to do but gave me a small task.

"Take this money, go out to the Farmer's market down the road and buy some eggs, butter, milk, sugar and flour," Mrs Axton announced as soon as I'd got into the kitchen. "Here is the list because I know you will forget."

Without a word, I took the list and the coins from her oily hand and bid her adieu. London was bright and sunny, unlike miserable Cardiff. People were bustling about, eager to find the cheapest sales.

"Twenty-five pennies for a clock! What a beauty! This one's rare I tell ya!"

"Jasmine all the way from India! Lavender as fine as gold! Buy your fresh cloth now!"

I stumbled past ladies and gents apologising as I went until I came to a stop at a big field with a striped tent in it.

The Circus! It wouldn't harm anybody just to use a few pennies for a little while...

I ran towards the big tent, eager to get inside when a broad man stopped me. He tutted, looking me up and down as he did so. For Pete's sake! Did everyone have to treat me like I was a dirty, homeless child?

"Money, please." His voice was low and growly, like a bear.

"Here," I said handing him a tuppence.

He tutted once more. "More."

"I haven't got any more."

"Yes you 'ave, you little liar!" the man cried, pointing to my leather bag.

"Ah, yes. But this money is for groceries, oh kind sir," I said, anxious to get into the circus.

Yet more tutting. "Well, Miss, I'm afraid you cannot come in. Terribly sorry."

"That's fine, sir, and maybe you should get your own tutting act, you'd be great!" Then I flounced off with my head high.

But I wasn't going back to Tippets house.

"Oh no!"

I was going to find a way into that circus, whether I had the money or not.

Twelve

The Circus

*quietly crept around to the back of the striped
tent. I lifted the fabric and slipped inside.

It was so noisy! Children were shouting
and clapping, their faces flushed with excitement as
acrobats were tumbling about the floor.

The circus was packed and there was nowhere
to sit. My legs soon started to get tired from
standing so I squeezed between a broad man and a
plump woman stealing half of their seats each so I
had a full one.

A young boy flipped around the floor. He was
very good but he kept doing the same tumbles. I
eventually got bored of him showing off his moves
and slipped through the bustling crowds and used
my money to buy myself a gingerbread. It reminded
me of Daisy and how we had become un-friends. I
missed Mircove Beach — and Daisy and Frank.

After the acrobat had finished, a young woman with jet-black hair and a dazzling smile entered the circle. She grinned and waved, then climbed up a ladder, which led to a thin piece of rope.

"Now, The Marvellous Marie will walk the high wire rope!" a man with a rather large whip announced. I was instantly in awe of her. She walked across the rope effortlessly, as if she was taking an evening stroll. Then, she started jumping on it! I clapped until my hands were sore.

The rest of the acts were good enough but none as grand as The Marvellous Marie. I watched comic tramps, more tumblers and horse-riders but they just failed to amuse me.

When all the acts finished and bowed, I suddenly remembered I was meant to go to the market and get the things for Mrs Axton. I ran out of the tent as fast as my legs would take me.

"Oi! You are that wretch who I said couldn't come in!" the man who tutted too much shouted. "Hey! Get back here, I'm not done with you yet!"

I kept running. Outside, it was getting dark and there were only a few market stalls left — none of which was selling the groceries Mrs Axton had asked for.

Great. My first full day and I was already in terrible trouble. I hung my head and started trudging back to Tippets House when I heard a high-pitched cry. It was like a little baby crying for help. I knew I should've just gone back to Tippets House if I didn't want to get into any more trouble but I couldn't exactly leave him — or her — whatever gender it was there all alone at night.

I followed the crying until the sound got louder and louder. It seemed like the cry was coming from under an abandoned market stall. I looked around just to make sure the owner of the stall wasn't anywhere near then I lifted up the cloth covering the stall.

"Oh my…"

In a tiny cage was a kitten. It cried out and pushed itself to the back of the cage.

"It's OK. I won't hurt you. Come here puss…" I held out my hand. The kitten was black with deep green eyes. Its eyes looked as if it was going to cry and that melted my heart. The poor thing also looked hurt. It was raising its paw which looked distorted and the kitten looked so starved you could see its ribs through its thick black fur. I poked my head out once more to be safe then scooped up the cage and ran all the way back to Tippets House.

* * *

The door was left open so I pushed on it as quietly as I could and ran into the kitchen, eager to put the kitten inside my room where it would be safe.

"Where are the groceries, Anya?" Mrs Axton asked, startling me as I walked into the kitchen.

"Uh — Well..." I thought about some plausible excuses; I got beaten up by thieves who stole the money. That I was forced to give up my money. Or, that I needed to run for my life. I decided that the second of the three sounded the most believable.

"Yes. Two men forced me to give them the money; I didn't want to but they took it!" I fake cried. I was actually very convincing.

"I see. I'm so sorry to say that..."

"Yes?" I interrupted.

"That you'll have extra chores tomorrow for lying to me!"

"I'm not lying..."

"Listen, girl. I'm not playing games with you. I've waited five hours just to see you come back with blimmin' nothing!"

"I am sorry, Mrs Axton but — I got carried away. It will not happen again."

"Well, sorry isn't going to get me my groceries! You know what, no supper for you tonight!"

"Please, Mrs Axton. I apologise!" I pleaded.

"Go! Now!"

I walked out the cold room as the second skivvy maid sniggered behind me.

Once alone in my bare, lifeless room, I removed the cage with the kitten inside it from under my bed. Its eyes were partially closed as if it had been sleeping.

I poked my finger through the bars and tried to stroke its smooth coat but it moved to the back of the cage and it curled itself into a little ball of fluff.

I bet it was hungry. Quietly, I crept out of my room and into the kitchen. Mrs Axton and the other maid weren't there so I snuck into the pantry. There was a tin of half-used tuna which I hid in my apron and tiptoed back to my room in the attic.

"Here you go little one," I said scraping out the tuna and placing it into the cage.

The kitten eyed the fish as if were some sort of wild beast then looked up at me. After a minute or so, hunger gave in and it started gobbling up the tuna. I watched it do so for a while then closed my eyes and snuggled into my *very* uncomfortable bed. Maybe I could try and prise the cage open with some sort of tool but that was for another day. I thought of Tad. I was still furious with him. Livid in fact, but Mam-gu had been right. No matter how difficult things were at home, he was still my Tad and I'm sure I would have been better off back with him. Who knows, things might get better. I thought I ought to write letters to Tad and Mam-gu but I was so drained, the only thing I could do was sleep.

Thirteen

A New Friend

*I*decided to make it up to Mrs Axton. Even though I wasn't one to be servile with others, I resolved that spending her money on no good wasn't right.

Before leaving, I looked around my small room for the kitten. I couldn't see it. I searched frantically in every corner of my room, not that there was much space to look around to start with.

It wasn't there. I started to panic. I'd fantasised about raising the little thing and sneaking it little bits of food and milk. The thought of eventually having my very own pet pleased me no end.

Running into the kitchen, I called, "Mrs Axton!"

"Blimey, what's all that horrible shouting?" Mrs Axton asked walking in.

"Where's my kitten?" I asked, almost crying.

"Your what? Get to work, Anya. I have no time for your games."

"You took away my kitten!" I choked.

"That scrap of a thing you call a kitten? Barely any meat on it."

I stared at her for several moments.

"You — you ate it…?" I whispered in disbelief, my eyes stinging.

"What? No! Can you really see me picking up my silverware, spreading my napkin and eating a cat? An excuse for a cat I might add. I threw the runt out. You are at work here Anya, no room for pets. Even if there was, that runt was probably carrying cholera and I'm not having that in this house."

The words "You horrible, spiteful woman!" seemed to leave my mouth of their own accord. As a soon as I'd said it, I covered my mouth but the damage was done.

Mrs Axton was furious. She closed the gap between us quickly and glowered at me so forcefully that I felt roasted. I could almost hear the hair in her nostrils dance with the movement of her breath.

"You try that again and you'll be more sorry than you've ever been in your life you hear me!" She sent me off to work with only scraps for breakfast and didn't let me off after that either. She made me scrub and wash the floors, a job Maud and I were supposed to share, change *all* the bed linen and empty the fireplaces. By the time I'd finished, I was hot, sweaty, exhausted and covered in soot. To trump it all my heart was heavy — I missed Cardiff and I missed my mam even more. How was life ever going to get better?

Around lunchtime, I decided to slip out of Tippets House for some fresh air. Making sure Mrs Axton was busy, I gently opened the back door and fled.

I hadn't the faintest clue where I was going but I kept on walking till I hit the market. Carrying on, I happened upon a bookstall, much to my delight. I'd brought with me some of the money Mam-gu had given me and ended up spending it all right away. There were such a huge variety of books to choose from! After several rounds of choosing then changing my mind then choosing again, I found the perfect book: *The Woman in White*. Despite the sadness of Tippets House, it filled me with gratitude that I had a mam-gu like mine. Without her, I wouldn't have been able to buy the little moments of joy the book was bound to bring.

* * *

As I was walking away merrily with my new book, I spotted a young boy, about eight or nine I would say, leaning against a brick wall. Like a lion's mane, his hair was untamed and his clothes were tattered — hardly suitable to wear and the soles of his shoes had come clean off.

"Please Miss, any spare change?" The boy looked up at me with sad, wistful eyes. I rummaged through my purse before realising I had spent all the money on my book. I looked at the boy then at my book, then back again.

"Come with me," I offered him my hand but he just stared at it with a blank expression on his face.

"Take my hand," I encouraged.
Gingerly, he stretched out his bony fingers and wrapped his hand against mine. His grasp was tight as if he never wanted to let go. I led him back to the bookstall. The owner was already packing the stall away so I ran up to him.

"Sorry missus," he said, "I'm packing away now."

"Yes, I can see that," I said in my head.

"May I please return this book in exchange for my money?"

"What's wrong with it?" the man asked, taking the book from me, "the spine seems to be holding up alright and there's no problem with the front or back cover."

"The book's wonderful sir, but I would like to buy something else please," I said as courteously as I could.

"Well, I don't know…"

"Please, sir!" I opened my eyes wide and batted my eyelashes.

"Alright, alright," he said, finally giving in, "but don't you go telling tales about refunds, you hear?"
I nodded and swapped my book for the money.

"Now let us go and find you some food." I pulled the boy along the now-quiet aisle of the market until we found a small stall selling fruits, vegetables and meats. Fortunately, they had not yet packed their goods away for the day.

The stall owner was small and frail. She was rocking back and forth hypnotically on a wooden chair.

"Hello," I said.
The old woman shut her eyes.

"Hello!" I repeated.

"Dearie me, what's all that ruckus?" she declared, sitting up.

"My, look how late it is! What brings you 'ere lovelies?"
She smiled; a kind but crooked smile.

"Well," I started, "I was hoping I could buy an apple?"

"Of course!" the old woman held out her hand for my money which I gave her.

She then picked out an apple digging her grimy nails into its juicy flesh. I winced but my new friend looked thrilled.

"Thank you very much," I said before walking off with the boy.

Much obliged, miss!" he said with a mouthful of apple. "Can we play a game?"

"A game?" I asked.

"Yes. How about tag?"

"I think I've forgotten how to play," I admitted forlornly realising my childhood was slipping away.

"It's okay, I'll teach you!" He shoved the rest of the apple into his mouth. "I run, and you try and catch me — simple."

"I never quite caught your name," I said before playing.

"Oh, well, I'm George. What is your name?"

"Anya," I replied.

"That's a pretty name," George responded.

"Thank you," I said, pleased.

George ran around the streets while I tried to catch him. I was not entirely sure it was the safest game but as it was getting dark, not many people were roaming about.

He was incredibly fast, and I had to keep stopping to catch my breath.

"Come tag me!" He'd say then zoom off whenever I came close.

Eventually, I managed to sneak up behind George and tag him.

By this time, it was getting very dark, so I said to George, "I better be off now. I hoped you liked the apple."

"Thank you so much, Anya!" he hugged me so hard I swear I heard a crack in my ribcage.

"Maybe I'll see you around again?" he asked, wistfully.

"Maybe, George. Good-bye!" I waved as I ran off down the street.

* * *

I slipped back into Tippets House as quietly as I could, but my efforts were in vain as waiting for me at the door, was Mrs Axton.

"Out gallivanting, were we?" she asked, arms folded, "Charity's room and the kitchen need cleaning and the table needs to be set, Anya!"

"I'm sorry Mrs Axton but I needed some air so I went for a walk. I had the best fun with a street boy. His name was George and..."

Without warning, Mrs Axton suddenly slapped me about the head — hard enough to make me see stars.

"Oww!" I exclaimed, holding my sore head.

"You stupid girl!" Mrs Axton roared, "First the cat and now a street kid and I bet he's from Spitalfields as well. Do you want to bring flamin' cholera into this house?"

"The what?" I questioned.

"That plague that's been going around. It's a sneaky thing — you never know you have it until you die."

I stared at the floor.

"Charity's already come down with something terrible, Anya! You're lucky I don't have the heart to chuck you out on the streets!" she said, stepping closer.

"Please no!" I cried stepping back with my hands over my face, quivering in fright.

"Get to your room, you urchin!"

Sitting alone in my room for a long while, I felt so very melancholy. The dingy room was made even worst by the fact that there was hardly time to clean it. I had no one to talk to or no one who would listen. No friends — nothing. What sort of life was this?

Then it occurred to me.

Mam-gu!

Mam-gu could always cheer me up.

It would take two weeks before it got to her and maybe a month before I heard back but what choice did I have?

"Paper and pen!" I thought aloud before scolding myself for being so noisy.

But where to get it from?

There was some paper in the kitchen and I'm sure I'd brought a pen with me. I hate the dark though and the idea of running out into the pitch-black kitchen was frightening.

I breathed in. I could do this. I needed to talk to somebody, to let it all out, or I would go mad.

I took one reluctant step after another into the jet-black unknown. I hadn't dared to take the lamp in case I woke somebody.

The only sound was my footsteps against the cold cobblestone floor and that alone sent shivers up my spine.

I was in the middle of the kitchen now, but I'd forgotten where the paper was.

I panicked at the thought of stepping on cockroaches which would undoubtedly be scuttling about on the dark floor as I started to swivel around, squinting through the inky nothingness.

"Anya?"

Thank the lord for Mrs Axton — however cruel and spiteful she might be.

"Thank God!" I exclaimed.

"What on earth are you doing up?" Mrs Axton had a candle in her hand and was wearing a pink nightdress, which made me want to giggle uncontrollably.

Miss. A pink nightie! Nothing was more chalk and cheese than that sight.

"I was going to the WC," I lied making a note of where the sheets of paper lay.

"Well, you'd best take this candle with you," Mrs Axton offered, "and be quick — I need to get back to sleep — and I don't want you trailing around like a ghost tomorrow."

"Thank you," I said sliding past her whilst deftly taking a sheet of paper with me.

* * *

As I traipsed back to my room, it struck me that giving me the candle was a sweet thing to do — the first act of kindness Mrs Axton had shown me during the entire time I'd been at Tippets House. Might Mrs Axton's personality have been switched during the night?

Once I was safely back in my room, I started writing to Mam-gu. It crossed my mind that it was going to be quite a mission to sneak out and get the letter posted, but I decided to cross that bridge when I got to it.

Dear Mam-gu,

How are you faring? I hope you have been keeping well. My time here at Tippets has been awful! I've not been here for two weeks yet but it feels like two years. At least writing you this letter brings some joy and conjures fond memories. I miss you Mam-gu — and Cardiff. Of course, I also miss Tad, although I'm still mad at him for sending me here. Will he come to his senses, I wonder? I haven't written to him yet because I am still so cross, but I do worry and hope he is well.

I was so very nearly late for the train here but fortunately — or unfortunately actually — I managed to jump on at the last moment. I had to sit next to an old wheezy man who kept offering me peppermints. Luckily, he got off at Gloucester.

London is huge, Mam-gu! Was New York like this? It is busy, bustling and full of bad-mannered people. I thought Queen Street in Cardiff was something. When I got to Paddington Station I was in awe, and imagine that's only one part of London! You'll never guess what Mam-gu — I was given a ride in a petrol-driven horseless carriage — from Paddington to Tippets House! It was a strange but wonderful contraption and it moved so quickly! Another strange man drove this marvel and he had the nerve to ask me if I was aged six! Not to worry Mam-gu, I gave him a good telling off!

When I arrived at Tippets house, I was welcomed — well, it was hardly a welcome — by a nasty lady by the name of Mrs Axton. She is a broad woman with big hands for whacking people with and a cold heart. Just today, she beat me black and blue for helping a hungry boy on the street! I work all hours the Lord sends with very little time off — even on Saturdays and Sundays.

I work closely with another scullery maid, a mean snob called Madeline, though she insists I call her Maud. She's got it in for me the wretched girl. I don't know what I ever did to her but I try my best to steer clear of her.

The master and mistress of Tippets House are pleasant enough. Their names are Master and the Mistress Edward. That is what I must call them as I do not yet know their names. They have a young daughter named Charity who is a *bit strange but easy to be fond of. She loves to play with dolls and spends most of her time doing so.*

Oh, there is the butler Charles who is rather sweet. He welcomed me with open arms and spoke at some length to me. I don't see him often though which is a little upsetting for he is the one kind face around here.

I really do not like it here Mam-gu. Please bring me home.

With my love regards,
Your Anya.

Fourteen

Lies

"**Y**ou are late!" Mrs Axton barked in my ear.

I jerked, stifling a yawn in the process. How was it already past dawn — and long had I slept?

Quickly getting out of bed, I put on my scratchy maid's uniform. Oh, yes. I didn't mention the 'clothing.' It was scratchy and tight. So tight, in fact, I could barely breathe. I had to snip a slit in both armpits for a bit of reprieve.

"Today, you will take Master Edward his breakfast," Mrs Axton instructed whilst I spooned up the last of my porridge. As I finished washing up my bowl and turned to leave, Maud tripped me and I fell into her.

"Careful, you clumsy thing!"

"I am being careful!" I yelled back, "Plus if you had looked where you were going, I would not have bumped into you!"

"Shh!" Mrs Axton hissed, pointing straight at me. "No shouting in the hallways you buffoon!"

"It wasn't just m..." She shot me a fierce look.

"Ugh!"

I stomped upstairs with the breakfast tray, cursing under my breath.

Halfway down the hall, I knocked on Master Edward's door but there was no answer. He normally studied in his room when he broke fast in the mornings, so it was a surprise he didn't appear to be there.

I tried calling out his name. "Master Edward?"

Still nothing. I took the risk and opened the door. The room was empty.

Closing the door silently, I crept back down the stairs having decided to look about the house; he'd have to be somewhere.

He wasn't anywhere — I searched the dining room, the drawing-room and library until my legs ached and my arms felt as if they could fall off from carrying the heavy breakfast tray.

Reluctantly, I headed back through the hallway about to give up and tell Mrs Axton what had happened. Just as I passed the living room, I caught sight of Master Edward sitting on the floor — crying.

"Master Edward?" I cautiously approached him.

"Anya? I, um..." Master Edward stood up and quickly wiped his eyes.

"Is everything alright?" I asked him.

"Yes, yes. Thank you. Now back to work. And you didn't see any of this. Is that clear?" He said motioning with his hands at what I presumed was the unfortunate situation in which I had found him.

"Yes, of course, Master Edward."

I set his tray down on the side stool, bobbed my head at him and made my way back to the kitchen, wondering what on earth that was about.

"Well, that took you an hour and a half didn't it?" Maud asked rudely, scrubbing the rusty pots.

"I've only just been able to find him, so keep your mouth shut. Where's Mrs Axton?"

"She's gone out to the market. Why? What's it to you anyway?" Maud inquired.

"Am I not allowed to question?"

"You can keep your questions to yourself or ask Mrs Axton when you see her!" Maud shouted.

What one earth did she have against me? I felt she needed a good lesson. A prank that would teach her some humility. However, I held back any such thoughts, partly because I did not want to get into any *more* trouble, and in all honesty, Maud's foul attitude was her problem, not mine. Thankfully, Maud finished and went about her other chores. I could certainly do with tidying the pantry in peace.

A while later, she reappeared. "Master Edward's mam's in the drawing-room. You must tend to her."

"How about *you* tend to her, Maud. I seem to be doing the best part of the work around here," I retorted.

"Well, I'm going to be washing up, Anya, and you currently have no work to be doing so be off with you."

Realising this was a battle I couldn't win, I trudged toward the drawing-room.

One of its big windows was open letting in the fresh air. I soaked it in. Being stuck in the bowels of Tippets House for most of the day meant that fresh air was a luxury. A red patterned rug lay on the floor. Cabinets holding dishes and cutlery stood guard around the room and a small coffee table covered with a white embroidered cloth proudly stood in the middle of several comfortable-looking chairs.

An old woman, slightly older than Mam-gu, sat confidently in one of the chairs, looking out the window. She had fine clothes, well-coiffed hair and a regal air about her. Her head turned sharply as she heard me walk in.

"Finally, I've been losing my marbles sat here," she said.

"Sorry, Ma'am," I responded, apologising and curtseying.

"Well, don't leave me parched and ravenous, get me a cup of tea and some biscuits."

Scurrying off to the kitchen, I busied myself making tea, not sure whether to put in one sugar or two. I lined the saucer with two biscuits and returned to the drawing-room.

"Here you are, Ma'am." I set down the plate on the coffee table. She sipped her tea, her beady eyes on me.

"What do they call you, eh?" she asked, "you must have *some* name."

"Yes, Ma'am. I am Anya Rees."

"Rees?" she asked, "sounds almost as strange as you look." I shifted from foot to foot uncomfortably. "What on earth are you wearing, Anya?"

Looking down at my uncomfortable, scratchy uniform, I replied, "this is my uniform ma'am."

"You may call me Lady Edwards and you may as well be wearing a noose. This is hardly suitable for a young girl to wear!" she exclaimed.

"I agree, Lady Edwards. I do not think much of it either."

"Hmph. Well, someone should see to it that whoever's making you wear that monstrosity gets a good check-up. That'll be all. Now leave me."

* * *

Halfway through chopping vegetables for lunch, I decided to put the parsnips on to start cooking. Near the stove, I spotted half a crown on the floor. Maud must have noticed it too as she turned, I could practically see shillings in her eyes.

"Must be Mrs Axton's money. I'll return it to her," I said, bending down to pick it up.

"No don't worry, I will," gushed Maud, quickly snatching it up.

For a moment the look in Maud's eyes made me question whether she *would* return it. I doubted Maud or anyone would ever have the nerve to steal from Mrs Axton. Or would she?

We fell into an almost easy silence and even some conversation as we prepared the rest of the lunch. Maud even filled me in a bit on Lady Edwards. In the middle of cutting up the lamb, Maud *hugged* me!

"Get off me, Maud." I pushed her away, surprised by the unusual gesture.

"Just a small gesture to a friend."

"Friend? You despise me! Let's not be fooled by this little truce here. I don't trust you."

"No, I don't."

"I'm back!" Mrs Axton was at the kitchen door before I could say anything more.

"Hello, dear Mrs Axton!" Maud chirped, cosying up to her. "I'll make you a nice cup of tea!"

"Thank you, Maud."

Why was Maud being so nice to Mrs Axton? Something was not right…"Maud dear, I lost half a crown this morning, do you know where it could've got to?"

"Well, I don't like to point fingers…" Maud giggled mischievously, "but I *did* see Anya pick something shiny up from the floor…"

I was outraged. "Me? You're the one who took it and I was the one who was going to *return* it!"
Maud pretended to look astonished. "I would never!"

"Well let's check pockets. Anya, come and stand here," Mrs Axton commanded and then dug her hands deep into my pockets; guess what she pulled out?

"You thief!" Mrs Axton declared. "And I was just getting to trust you!"

Maud's smug face was what I hated the most. Her eyes gleamed with maliciousness and the ends of her mouth twitched as she tried not to burst into fits of laughter.

"I did not take your money, I promise!" I protested.

"Then why was it in your pocket, Anya?" Maud asked.

"Maud, dear, I'll handle this. Then why was it in your pocket, Anya?"

"Maud must've put it in there!" I said.

"The nerve!" Maud gasped.

"Maud, I've got it. The nerve!" Mrs Axton repeated. "Anya, enough excuses. I really *do* need to look through your things. Who knows what else you could have stolen? How I wish the factories weren't poaching all the maids, we'd have had a dozen more maids better than you. No lunch or dinner for you. Assuming you can get on my good side in the morning I might not tell the Master of this shameful development. Now off with you!"

I stormed out of the kitchen and into the hallway, slamming the door behind me.
Suddenly, I heard a man's voice. "I'm sorry Edward."
I quickly crouched down, afraid of being seen.

"Is there not any way I can have a little more time? Please!" Master Edwards voice was full of pain.

"Edward, I feel for you, I really do but you've already had extended time. I'm afraid that if the money is not paid within the next few days, you will have to give up the house."

The remainder of the conversation consisted of murmurs, but I'm almost certain I could make out a sob from Master Edward. Closing the door, he went back upstairs as I hid in the shadows.

As I crept slowly into my room, I sympathised with Master Edward and wondered what losing Tippets House would mean for me.

Fifteen

Dinner For Eighteen And Life's Not Fair

❧

"**G**et up!" Mrs Axton shouted, shaking me from side to side.

"Argh!" I cried, jumping, "I'm up." I wish Mrs Axton's room was in another part of the house instead of just down the hall from mine. I could really do without her stopping by my room every morning to shake me out of bed! One of these days, I'd surprise her and be down in the kitchen working away by the time she woke up and came to perform her morning ritual of hollering in my ear.

"Will you get up, Anya?" Mrs Axton repeated, "You need to start early today."   "Why?" I asked. Wasn't the crack of dawn early enough, I mused?

163

"There's a sudden dinner party to be catered for. Madam told me late yesterday afternoon she wanted enough food for eighteen!" Mrs Axton fumed, "she must have been tipsy!"

"Madam's not tipsy," I said, rubbing my eyes and sitting up.

"How'd you know? You've hardly met her. She must be tipsy if she thinks we're going to have dinner ready in time for *eighteen*," Mrs Axton exclaimed. "Let's just pray to the Lord that we can do it, or we'll all be out on our ears. It doesn't help if you continue lying there like you own the place — get up!"

I hate Mrs Axton.

Reluctantly, I got up and put on my uniform.

"Finally!" Mrs Axton cried as I trudged into the kitchen.

"You're lucky I did the difficult bits last night. Now, don't just stand there like you are deaf and dumb — to work with you!"

"Where's Maud?" I questioned. She was accustomed to this life and was usually up early to get some of her chores out the way.

"The poor girl has taken ill," Mrs Axton stated, looking worried. "She won't be working today, so you will carry the bulk of her jobs."

I had to help make the pudding, but I was horrid at it and ended up burning the desert.

"You clumsy thing!" Mrs Axton said, pushing aside. She quickly removed the burnt remnants of plum pudding.

"Go and make yourself useful. There's loads to do yet. I know it's rather too much for you today, but the floors need cleaning."

"Do I have to?"

"The cheek on you! I'll give you 'Do I have to?' If I wasn't a respectable lady, I would teach you a harsh lesson for talking back to me on a day like this," Mrs Axton quipped.

I wonder who had lied and told her that she was respectable? Feared maybe! Definitely not respectable. At least not to me anyway.

So, I ended up washing the floors, which was awful. Maud came through from the pantry looking a bit like death warmed over. I ventured a greeting which she either ignored or didn't hear. I thought best to leave her be. What the matter was with her obviously wasn't helping her mood.

"You should be in bed Maud," Mrs Axton puffed as she laid out the serveware.

"I feel somewhat better; I could help serve."

It was quite convenient, Maud feeling better just in time for the guests to arrive. She was obviously keen not to miss out on the arrivals. To be honest, I was excited too.

* * *

After much sweat, blood and tears, everything was ready for the dinner party. We stood a safe distance away peeking at the front door through the crack of the door leading to the hallway. People had just started arriving. There was a distractingly tall man with a very tall top hat and long shoes. Everything about him was tall. I'd bet if I could see his toes, they would be tall and all! Another guest arrived — a lady looking very regal in her purple dress. Mrs Axton peeked out of the kitchen door and gasped.

"That dress is just past her knees, it's ridiculous!"

"I think she looks rather grand if you ask me," I said.

"Well nobody asked you," Maud said bluntly.

I stuck my tongue out at her and she did the same. A bell in the kitchen suddenly rang.

"That'll be Mistress Edwards," Mrs Axton said.

"Make sure you're ready as this will probably be your first time."

"My first time for what?" I questioned.

The bell rang again.

"Quick now, she's not very patient," Mrs Axton gushed, ushering me up the stairs.

I knocked.

"Come in."

I walked in and quickly went to walk out again.

166

"Hold on child, it's only me. Help me with my corset, will you." Mistress Edwards made me stand behind a very strange looking pulling machine.

"Use this to go around and around. Do not stop until I say so."

I grabbed hold and started going around. She started grunting so I faltered but she told me to keep going until...

"Stop!"

Phew! My arms felt like jelly.

"Thank you, dear. Now could you fetch me my gown; I'm not sure if I can move in this thing," she said.

"Would you like me to make it looser Ma'am?" I asked.

"No, no. I'm quite alright, thank you."

I handed her the gown, then bobbed my head and left to return downstairs.

"How was it?" Mrs Axton asked me as I walked into the kitchen.

"Horrible! My arms feel like jelly," I replied.

"Well it's not exactly going to be easy," Maud offered, laughing.

"Nobody invited your opinion," I said facing up to her.

"You two!" Mrs Axton pulled me away from Maud, my cheeks red. "You fight like cats and dogs.

Now stop this silly behaviour and let's serve the food."

I was charged with carrying the lamb to the dining room. It was very noisy in the room as the boisterous men guffawed and the women gossiped. Maud and I eventually got all the food onto the table and Mrs Axton asked us to take our places in the corner of the room in case anyone needed anything.

Maud wasn't overly impressed with the idea. She muttered angrily under her breath as she walked over to her corner, frowning.

Just to goad her, I smiled as if I was having the best time of my life. I wasn't. It was incredibly boring just standing there in the corner. I passed the time by humming songs in my head.

After a while, a kind-looking lady beckoned me over to her. "Hello, dear," she said, "could you please pass me two slices of bread."

"Of course, m'lady. Your plate please."

She handed me her plate and I got her two slices of bread from the other side of the long dining table.

"Thank you, my lovely. And may I just say how awful that young girls frown looks? My, my! Her face is nearly as long as a horses snout — it's bound to put me off my food!"

I chuckled but then quickly stopped, afraid of embarrassing myself or getting into trouble.

"Here child, take this. At least it'll keep you going for a bit after waiting on us so long." The kind lady handed me something wrapped in a paper napkin.

"Are you sure m'lady?" I asked.

She nodded.

"Thank you so much," I gushed.

"Make sure you suck it and let it melt around your mouth. That way, you'll be content for a little while," the lady advised.

I wanted to hug her. I couldn't remember the last time I had anything sweet. I went back to my corner popping the sweet into my mouth before I turned around to face the room. I let the sticky slime from the toffee coat my tongue, filling me with glee. But nothing good lasts forever. Before long, no matter how much I tried to stretch it, the sweet dissolved into nothingness.

After a while, standing in that corner, I thought that I might become bored out of my mind. Thankfully, the guests finally started leaving the table. It was mine and Maud's cue to start gathering up plates and the remnants of the food, but Maud didn't show any sign of moving so I shook her and hissed, "Maud... Maud!"

"I can hear you! I wouldn't be sleeping on my feet would I. Get off me!" Maud snarled.

"If you say so," I laughed. "Now come on, these dishes won't wash themselves."

Maud and I gathered plates and cutlery and took them all back to the kitchen whilst Master and Mistress Edwards saw the guests out.

Finally, we got everything off the dining table and into the kitchen.

"I'll wipe the table," Mrs Axton said. "I must say you girls have done a wonderful job today. Anya, how about you grab some carrots to boil from the vegetable cupboard and Maud put some water in that big pot over there."

"Whatever for?" I asked Mrs Axton.

"To cook you in," Maud cackled.

"Now, now Maud, be nice. There's no point putting all this good food to waste is there Anya? And they've hardly eaten a single scrap of it."

I agreed and got a few carrots from the cupboard and threw them into the pot, which was now full of boiling water.

"Right, it's a third of a chicken; we'll each get a decent slice, then we can move onto the pork, then the…" Mrs Axton went on and on about all the food.

She was right, it would have been a shame to let the food go to waste. We had a feast. I was so stuffed, I could barely walk!

"My corset's about to pop!" Mrs Axton gasped, "I feel like the bloomin' queen eating all this chow."

"I agree," I said. "I think I'm going to go to bed now. Goodnight."

"Me too," Mrs Axton said. "My stomach's fit to bursting." Sat on my bed, I thought the day hadn't been so bad after all.

Whatever the case, I couldn't shake how much I missed Mam. I wanted one of her tight, warm hugs. I was interrupted by a soft double knock at my door.

"Come in, I called."

It was Maud of all people.

"What do you want Maud? I'm not in the mood for your nastiness or lies. I just want to get some sleep," I said.

"I want to talk, Onio... I mean Anya."

"Talk? Why do you want to talk to me? You hate me."

"Shh! You'll get us both into trouble," Maud said sitting down on the end of my bed.

"Listen, Maud, I don't..."

"Just shut up and listen to me. I'm sorry for blaming you for stealing and I'm sorry for being horrible and nasty to you. My family is very, very poor and when I saw that money, I had to take it. But I was wrong to try and pass the blame when Mrs Axton came in asking for it before I had a chance to leave the kitchen. I need this job as it means I can help my family. This was the only place willing to accept me as the others said I have a bit of a cheek about me."

"Well they're not wrong," I offered.

171

"I'm serious," Maud said, "And I'm terribly sorry for, well, everything."

I was shocked. Maud had not said a kind word to me since I'd arrived at Tippets House. I stayed silent for a while then said, "Well, as long as you promise to stop being so mean. It really is unnecessary."

"I'll try, I promise."

Where's your family anyway and how did you come to Tippets House?"

"My family lives in Newcastle but they don't have much. Hardly enough for me and my siblings to be fed with anyway. So I send some money back from my wages to help keep them going. What about you?"

My Tad and Mam-gu live in Cardiff. There's not really much to tell. I should be getting to bed now."

Maud looked forlorn as she left my room. I did feel sorry for her but it had been too much of a long day to dwell on it now. As soon as my head hit the pillow, I fell asleep.

Sixteen

Drunk Men Like Dancing Girls

⚬⟞⟜⟞⟜⟞⟜⟞⟜⟞⚬

"Anya, hurry up with the sweeping," Mrs Axton's harsh voice called as I rubbed my tired eyes. It had been another long day already and I had woken up tired.

My bed hardly made for a good night's rest. Two days had passed since the dinner party and I still didn't feel rested. It didn't help that since the dinner, Maud had taken to her bed, not helping out much.

"After that, you've got the mopping and the dusting to do so I 'spose you best be getting a move on."

"Why can't Maud help out with something?" I asked.

"You hateful little rat! The poor girl's sick to her stomach and she can hardly breathe let alone move!"

"I'm so sorry, I forgot." I was ashamed.

"Well, Anya, try not to forget when people are close to their death." Mrs Axton clasped her mouth and with glazed eyes ran into the kitchen. I felt sorry for Maud and it wasn't right to complain so I decided to visit her.

I had never been in Maud's room before. As I climbed to the attic, I didn't really know what to expect, but her room was a lot like mine.

The room was just about as big as a box and had very little in it. Maud had somehow found some cabinets to put up. Little china dolls were arranged by colour so all the ones with pink dresses were on the left and those in green on the right.

On the floor, lay a thin mattress with a very ill-looking girl on it.

"Oh, Maud." I sat down beside her and stroked her head.

I had never shown this much or any affection for that matter towards her, but seeing her in this state broke my heart.

Her face was red. Yes, red. Bright red spots, masses of them, swarmed her skin. Maud's eyes fluttered open as she whispered, "Stay off me." I smiled. Even though dangerously ill and despite her apology she could still hate me.

"Don't come near, Anya. You'll catch it."

I stepped back, "How did you get this, Maud? Whatever it is."

"It's scarlet fever," Maud coughed, "My Mam had it and she died."

"Maud, I'm so sorry. I know how it feels."

"No, you don't. She was the only one I had. I was sent here to try and earn some money for all my brothers back home. They're all alone."

Maud's eyes were glassy, and I felt the urge to hug her, but I didn't want the illness that her mam had died from.

"Leave me..." Maud sighed and closed her eyes. A sign which meant *go away, Anya.*

My head was bursting with questions, but I left Maud in peace. I didn't know what to do. I was too much in a state of sad shock to go back to my chores, so I decided to go out.

My purse was just about empty, holding just a few silver coins. *That might be enough to buy me hot cocoa* I thought. The early evening air was fresh and breezy and hardly anyone was about. The leaves were rustling in the trees above and the sky was dimming due to the setting sun. I hadn't the faintest clue which sort of shop would sell hot drinks, so I tried a small building a short walk away from Kingstone Road. It looked like an alehouse, so I thought to try my luck. The alehouse Tad went to sold hot cocoa. As soon as I walked in, my ears started to buzz from the loud music being played. The alehouse was crammed with people — some old and some not much older than me. Young boys and men were moving rhythmically about as the young girls and *women* frolicked and danced flamboyantly. Mrs Axton would surely have complained! The musical celebrations were in full swing. I attempted to leave, realising there would be no hot cocoa on offer here, but a young man, not much older than me, pulled me into the middle of the room. Everyone stared at me and I could feel my cheeks burning. Then one fool decided to chant "Dance! Dance! Dance!" Soon, everybody was chanting it.

Well, I might as well I thought. I ripped off my ribbon so that my hair hung loosely around my shoulders.

The thing is, I have two left feet; put simply, I couldn't dance to save my life! I moved my body in ways I never previously imagined! I kicked my legs up and out, to the side and back not minding if anyone saw my undies. I moved in and out of rhythm and was soon jumping onto tables knocking over some chairs as I leapt. It felt like just what the doctor ordered; I was having such a grand time that I forgot all about Tippets House until...

"Anya!" Mrs Axton exclaimed, bursting through the doors. "What on earth are you doing here?"

"Mrs Axton! We've missed you. Glad to see you've eventually popped by again," a man with a long moustache shouted.

Mrs Axton almost turned bright pink. "What do you mean again?"

"That's a good one, Mrs Axton!" called a woman, laughing. "Back in the day, you and your old man visited so often you nearly lived here!" another woman added. Mrs Axton turned even pinker.

"I would never run riot with the likes of you," she exclaimed, and with that, she pulled me down from the table and dragged me out.

On the way back to Tippets House, she didn't say a word. I guess she was embarrassed, which amused me tremendously. I kept wondering who the man was that they were referring to. I was instructed to start on the supper whilst Mrs Axton looked after Maud. Thinking about Maud, I wanted to sneak a look at her, so a little later, I followed Mrs Axton discretely to her room. Mrs Axton had propped Maud up on a pillow and was spoon-feeding her hot soup.

"There now," she whispered soothingly as Maud struggled with swallowing. "It's all going to be alright."

Afraid of being caught, I slipped back into the kitchen to finish the supper. How was it that Mrs Axton could be so kind? If I wasn't any smarter, I would've thought she was a different person. Charles walked in, interrupting my thoughts.

"Charles! How lovely to see you!" It cheered me up to see him.

"You too, Anya," Charles said. "Have you seen Mrs Axton anywhere?"

"She's in with Maud," I replied. "Maud's come down with something horrific and Mrs Axton, believe it or not, is looking after her."

"You know, Anya, Mrs Axton isn't as nasty as she appears; she *has* got a soft side."

"Pfft," I laughed. "A soft side? Mrs Axton? Are we even talking about the same woman?"

"Don't be so quick to judge, Anya," Charles scolded gently.

"Everyone has a back story.

"Pray tell, Charles," I begged.

"I'm not sure it's really my place," he ventured.

"Please?"

"Well, if it'll help you understand…"

"Yes, it will!" I cried. I loved stories as much as a toddler would.

"Okay then," Charles said. "She wasn't always like this you know. I've worked with her here at Tippets House long enough to know. Some time ago,

Mrs Axton lived a happy enough life in an old cottage down in the south of London. She lived with her husband, Barry, and their two boys Liam and Sam. Barry worked here as a footman. They were such a jolly pair. With their two boys, they had enough to eat and drink, clean clothes to wear and a roof over their heads. Most of all, they were content. When she was off work, she sometimes helped out on the nearby farms in exchange for some food. Early one morning, she set off for eggs and for milk, basket and bucket in tow. Her boys hadn't been feeling too well with some sort of fever, but it didn't seem much to worry about. She left them with Barry thinking a quick trip down to the farm to fetch some food for the family would certainly help."

"Why have you stopped?" I asked, my imagination coming to a halt.

"I thought you might be bored," he said.

"Never!" I exclaimed, "I love stories. Carry on."

"Alright. So, Mrs Axton had been on the farm for a while when a neighbour came running up to her in the fields. 'Elizabeth,' she puffed, her face tight with worry. Mrs Axton turned, wondering what her neighbour had come all this way for. She told that her Liam and Sam had taken a turn for the worse; Liam was vomiting violently and had diarrhoea and Sam felt as though he was burning up when touched. Mrs Axton ran home faster than an eagle could fly, so stricken with worry that she was dripping with sweat from head to toe. When she reached home, her boys — well, they had come down with an illness that could not be cured. Mrs Axton would not tell me what it was. By all accounts, I think they had both caught smallpox. What she did say was that it was horrifying watching Liam and Sam go through it. Eventually, they died."

I sat in silence, processing Mrs Axton's heartbreaking story. "So, you see Anya?" Charles continued, "since then she's become entirely different from the cheerful woman she once was. She's afraid of opening up to anyone. She thinks she shouldn't have left them that day or could've been there quicker for her boys and saved their lives. She blames herself when in fact I doubt anyone was to blame. As for poor old Barry, he was left too devastated by it all and is hardly known to leave home these days."

"I'm so sorry," I said feeling a bit rotten. "I didn't realise Mrs Axton had another home."

"Well, don't apologise to me," Charles said.

"Her husband, Barry, now lives with his mother as they couldn't afford to keep her home. So Mrs Axton sees him on her days off. So, how about you be extra kind to Mrs Axton from now on, eh?"

I shamefacedly agreed as Charles left the kitchen. It wasn't long before Mrs Axton marched in.

"What happened to the supper, Anya?"

"So sorry, Mrs Axton. Just finishing it now."

"Excuse me?" Mrs Axton stated, looking flabbergasted.

"So sorr…"

"I know what you said, Anya. It's just — never mind."

For the remainder of the evening, I made sure I did my work out of Mrs Axton's way. It all seemed to be going to ruin at Tippets House. I was mostly left to my own devices to finish supper and serve Master and Mistress Edwards, something I didn't feel ready for at all. Clearing up after dinner, I overheard the Mistress Edwards in the drawing-room saying,

"I need to go to the children's hospital to be with Charity, dear. I shall spend the night there if they let me. Hopefully, it won't be long before she's back home."

I felt terrible for Charity. I thought it was bad slaving away all day, but there she was having to battle with being terribly sick with God knows what. First Charity, then Maud. I wondered if Charity also had scarlet fever and whether she had given it to Maud. It all seemed to be going downhill and felt terribly sad and suffocating at Tippets House.

* * *

The next day, I looked in on Maud before heading downstairs. She looked worse. I didn't think that was possible and it scared me stiff seeing her lying there looking so listless. I wondered how Charity was doing, hoping for some good news for a change. At least she was in the hospital. Poor Maud had to battle scarlet fever with hot soup and cold compresses up in her attic room. It hardly seemed fair. I needed some space. Mrs Axton, believe it or not, let me go out for a *walk*. Yes, a walk!

I headed for Kingstone market. The hustle and bustle were bound to cheer me up. The market was open and extremely busy with men shouting to market their goods, women 'oohing and aahing' over brocade and satins, and children squealing with delight as they received new toys. I wished I could be a child again, carefree without a worry in the world.

Further into the market, I saw a little girl making things out of paper. I so badly wished I had some money to throw into her little hat.

"Hello," a familiar voice called. I was greeted with a smile as I turned around.

"Hello there," I replied.

"Sorry, what was your name again?"

"George. You forgot already?"

"Ah, yes, George." Warning signs flashed as I remembered what happened the last time I played with George, but I dismissed the thought quickly. I badly needed the distraction. Life at Tippets House was becoming more and more unbearable with everyone dropping with sickness. I didn't even have Maud to fight with.

"This is my gang. He's Fred, short for Frederick and here's Lola, Ben and Vicky," George stated, as he introduced me to his friends and took a bow.

"What are you all doing here?" I inquired.

"Well, Fred, Ben and me are barrow boys. Lola and Vicky help out folk in the market with odd jobs. Spitalfields is getting too crowded. We don't get good tips there anymore."

George piped up. "Will you play with us?"

"What are you playing?" I asked him

"Horseshoes," Vicky told me

"You have to try and get the horseshoe around that stick. If you get it, you win," Ben said.

"Please play with us!" Lola begged.

"Oh, alright then," I said, grateful for the distraction.

The game was surprisingly fun. I managed — eventually — to get the horseshoe around the stick and the gang celebrated with me. All too soon it got late and I had to leave.

"This was quite a bit of fun. Thank you for letting me play with you," I said.

"No problem," George responded, winking, and I chuckled.

"Goodbye!" Lola said as I headed back to Tippets House.

"Bye," I waved.

"Where on this bloomin' earth did you get to, Anya? When I said you could go for a walk, I didn't mean to Timbuktu! You do know with Maud being sick and me looking after her half the time, there is no one else to tend to the rest of what needs doing around here?" declared Mrs Axton, back to her old self.

"You let me go for a walk on my break, Mrs Axton. I needed a bit of fresh air."

"A break? A quick walk is all I meant. Not a break." Mrs Axton looked amused. "Oh, us servants never take a break young lady. No, no. That's not for the likes of us."

I hated that. I never wanted to be *her* kind or Maud's kind or any other servant's kind.

"Well, I'll be more than just a lowly servant one day," I vowed.

"You? That's about as truthful as pigs flying," laughed Mrs Axton.

"You'll see," I muttered starting to walk away.

"Hey, come back here! I never said you could leave. A servant only rests when its bedtime and that's not any time soon."

* * *

Sneaking up to my room to catch my breath, I crashed onto my bed. I'd somehow managed to finish the never-ending list of work and I was exhausted. There seemed to be no let-up. If every day was going to be like this, I really could not live here any longer. But I knew I had to face the reality of the situation — I only had a few pennies and nowhere to go. I felt like screaming into my pillow at the unfairness of it all. One day I would be famous: perhaps a glamorous performer or a beautiful singer. I tried singing a couple of notes but immediately stopped due to the ruckus I was making! I sounded horrible!

"Anya, come here please," I heard Mrs Axton call.

Trudging downstairs to the laundry room, I responded with "Yes Mrs Axton, did you call?"

"Charity's back and you need to see that she gets washed and changed ready for bed."

I went upstairs and peeked my head around Charity's open bedroom door. The girl I saw wasn't the same Charity who had run about Tippets House playing with her dolls or singing happily to herself all day. Charity's once long, brown hair hung limp and thin on her shoulders. Her skin was so pale it was almost green and her eyes were emotionless, as though she was confused and had no clue as to where she was. The Mistress Edward was kissing her forehead as Master Edward held her hands.

"Don't just stand there gawping," Mrs Axton said, startling me. "Go in and give the poor girl a good scrub."

"Hello, Charity," I said, bending down to greet her.

She looked blankly at me.

"Let's go and have a wash, eh? Then we can play with your dollies." I took Charity's hand and led her to the bathroom.

"So — what was it like?" I ventured, taking off her dress.

Charity grunted as if saying *it was hell on earth.*

"Can you talk at all?" I asked.

Charity shuddered and started making muffled screaming sounds.

"Oh, Charity, I'm sorry. I didn't mean to get you all upset!" I said trying to calm her down.

Making sure not to make the temperature of the bathwater too hot or cold, I turned the taps on. I picked Charity up and lowered her gently into the bathtub. Gosh, she was as light as a waif. On a nearby shelf was a block of carbolic soap, which I lathered into my hands before giving her a good scrub. It was an awkward business but I made sure not to get any soap in her eyes or mouth before pouring water on her with a bucket to rinse the carbolic off. I dried her and I then creamed her skin with olive oil. Dressing was much more challenging because Charity wouldn't agree with anything I chose for her; she just sat on her bed and refused to pick a dress to wear.

"This one's lovely," I assured her.

Charity grunted angrily and threw the dress on the floor.

"Charity, why do you have to be so difficult?" I ranted feeling at the end of my tether.

As I turned back to her chest of drawers to find something else she might want, she started making small sniffling noises. I looked up to see that she was crying.

"Charity I..."

I gingerly sat next to her and put my arm around her bony shoulders.

"Charity, I *am* sorry. I know how dreadfully difficult it must be for you," I said to her.

"How about we put on this lovely dress?" I fetched her a pink dress adorned with little dogs around its hem. Charity managed a smile and acquiesced. Upon entering the front room, Mistress Edwards greeted me with "Well done Anya, dear," as she scooped up Charity and held her close.

"You've brought some colour back to those pale cheeks."

I nodded meekly and exited the room.

"Well, you did a number on Charity, didn't you?" Mrs Axton said, "A good number that is. At least she's not making those horrible sounds."

"Well, I sympathise with Charity," I stated.

Mrs Axton looked at me and then a few seconds later burst out laughing.

"*Well, I sympathise with Charity and I talk posh. How'd you do Miss Ferryweather!*" she mimicked, laughing heartily.

"It's not funny," I said.

"Don't get me wrong, Anya — we do sympa...whatever it is, but Charity is a tiresome child sometimes," Mrs Axton said in between fits of laughter.

I couldn't disagree. Charity wasn't exactly the easiest youngster to look after.

"No point dwelling on the past," Mrs Axton said, "Now let's get cracking because we've got dinner to make."

That night's dinner was going to be beef pie which was easy enough to prepare but we weren't so lucky with the pudding. Master Edward had instructed we make Charity's favourite — treacle tarts with clotted cream. I had no idea how to make treacle, but fortunately, Mrs Axton knew about every recipe ever created so it wasn't much trouble.

I plopped an extra spoon of jam onto Charity's tart. Mrs Axton saw me, but she didn't say anything. Something else to be thankful for I suppose. I'm sure she agreed that the poor girl needed fattening — not for Christmas or anything — but she badly needed some meat on her bones in general.

For the rest of the evening, I sat in my room contemplating the good and bad things about Tippets House; the good: Charity, the food of course and Charles, and the bad: just about everything else!

As I drifted off into an uneasy slumber, I thought of Mam. Her warm hugs, protective arms wrapped tightly around my body, and her beautiful face smiling down at me.

I miss you, Mam.

Seventeen

Enough Already!

❧

"Good job, Anya," Mrs Axton said as she spotted me sweeping the hallway.

"Thank you, Mrs Axton."

She really did seem to be thawing towards me. Since Charles told me what she'd been through with her children, I couldn't help but feel for her. I thought to myself, it's amazing how things change if only we know one more thing. Maud being so dreadfully ill could not be helping either. It wouldn't surprise me if Mrs Axton was having déjà vu constantly whilst she looked after Maud. On the subject of Maud, I couldn't wait for her to get better. Truthfully I would prefer it if we were bickering non-stop as long as she wasn't so unwell. Plus, let's admit it, the work was killing me. Thankfully, it was Friday. Saturdays and Sundays usually brought a breather; fewer chores to do and even less to do for Charity as they normally went to the country at the weekends. As she started to walk away I called, "Mrs Axton?"

"Yes."

"I'm sorry about your boys. But am sure it wasn't your fault."

She stood still, a blank look on her face. For a moment, I wondered if I had overstepped the mark. Why on earth had I blurted that out? She walked up to me. When she got close enough, I could see she looked as though she was on the brink of tears. Before I had a chance to think anything else, she wrapped her worn, strong arms around me; her grip was so fierce and tight anyone would be forgiven for thinking she was trying to kill me!

She cleared her throat, dusted down her apron and smiled a half sort of smile at me before retreating to the kitchen.

"Well, that just happened," I muttered.

Later that morning, I received a letter. As soon as I got a spare moment, I took it hurriedly into my room and ripped open the envelope.

My Darling Anya,

It's me, Mam-gu. I got your letter and was shocked but more than anything saddened by it. I thought you'd be having at least an alright time there, but you sound like your living a nightmare! So, it's pointless asking how you are unless things have drastically changed for the better in the two weeks since your letter arrived. The last thing I want for any grandchild of mine is to be holed up with nasty characters like that Mrs Axton and Maud you described in your letter. That did break my heart and bring a tear or two to my eyes.

Everything is right as rain here in Cardiff, though I am a tad lonely without you! But don't worry, we can fix that, I'm sure.

Your father has taken ill. Too much alcohol I expect. I've been round to see him once or twice — never mind that we're still anything but best mates. I'm sure he'll recover though, and I will send him your love.

Your uncles, aunties and cousins are all faring well too. Rose has been back for a visit from Bangor. She looked ever so grown and missed seeing you too. They were only down for a few days but it was jolly good to see them all.

Much love,
  Mam‑gu.

I read the letter again. What did she mean by 'We can fix that, I'm sure'? Could she possibly...?

I didn't and couldn't think about it long, as Tad was ill. Even though he had treated me terribly and failed me, he was still my Tad. There was no denying, I cared about him. I grabbed my trusty pen and paper and began writing.

Dear Tad,

It's me Anya, your daughter. I say that like you've forgotten! I miss you, Tad. I caught wind of the fact you have taken ill. I do hope you get better quickly and hope it's nothing serious. Promise me you will look after yourself. You must realise I only have one parent left — you.

Even though I am still cross with you for making me come here, I wish I could see you

193

again soon. I wasn't sure what I expected coming here, but things here are far worse; the hard labour especially is killing me.

There are so many challenges, trials and adventures I want to tell you about Tad, but I'm afraid they will tire you, so this will have to do.

Much love,
  Anya.

Looking at the letter, I scratched my head. It needs to be more sentimental, I thought. Not so straight to the point. I should have at least enquired about work and how he got on with food and other things. In the end, I posted the letter as it was. It was payday, so I could afford the postage, plus there was no point dilly-dallying only to end up missing the post for that day and having to wait until Monday to get the next chance; that would only prolong the desperate wait for the reply I knew would follow upon receipt of my letter.

Thinking about the long wait I had endured before hearing from Mam-gu or Tad about how he was, I wept. Right there and then. Hot tears spilt down my cheeks as I thought about Tad lying there, alone in a hospital bed surrounded by strangers.

"Hello?" Mistress Edwards walked in holding some sort of a bag wrapped tightly and tied with some red ribbon.

I was surprised she was down here at all. The Master or Mistress rarely came down to the lower level see what the servants were up to.

"Are you alright, dear?" she asked, advancing towards me. Quickly, I wiped my tears and responded with,

"I'm fine, thank you, Mistress Edwards."

"You don't look fine," she said, sitting down beside me on my mattress. That was another shock. What was going on? She actually sat down on my skanky old mattress!

"What's wrong?"

I couldn't hold it in — my troubles had been growing to the size of gas balloons and I was ready to expel the air! "I hate it here; Maud is ever so sick and Mrs Axton can be so nasty. Things are getting better but it doesn't help reading that my Tad has been taken quite ill plus my Mam-gu is in Cardiff missing me. Not only that, but this itchy uniform is also doing my head in. Sometimes, I wish I could rip it off. It gets so itchy it's hard to breathe." I covered my mouth, cursing myself.

"Sorry, I didn't mean to say that."

The mistress looked aghast for a moment before saying, "Don't worry... Anya? Am so sorry to hear

195

about your father. I hope he gets better soon and as for the work around here, I'm sure you'll become more accustomed as the days go by. I'll let you in on a secret, sometimes, I wish I could be shot of my regal dresses too, but alas, it cannot be so." I stared at her. The *Mistress* got tired of her fancy clothes?

"Well, the *real* reason I'm here is not to talk about our clothes, but to give you this."

She handed me the bag she had carried in with her and I looked down at it.

"Open it!"

I unwrapped the ribbon and opened the bag to find...

"A new uniform and a pretty sundress!"

"Yes. Lady Edwards mentioned in her very direct manner that your current one is a monstrosity," the Mistress said with a chuckle.

"And so, I had it made a couple of sizes bigger with a different fabric so it's not itchy and irritating. It's a little something to say thank you for looking after Charity so well since she got back home from the hospital." For a moment, I wondered what pill she'd taken to be so kind and generous to me. This was unusual. Very unusual. Then I remembered Mam warning me about staring a gift horse in the mouth. Whatever the case, my mood was definitely lifted.

"Oh, thank you!" I encased her with a hug before coming to my senses and pulling away.

"So sorry, m'lady."

"No worries, dear," she replied, "Enjoy it!"

Once she'd left, I pranced about my room, humming with my new sundress held up against me.

"What's all this racket, aye?" Mrs Axton asked as she barged into my room.

"Oh, isn't it wonderful, Mrs A?" I exclaimed, merrily showing off my new frock to her.

"Don't you go taking liberties and calling me 'Mrs A'. What 'ave you had to drink, Anya, eh? And where'd you get that atrocious gown from?"

"The Mistress!" I cried, "She gave it to me. Oh, joy! No more scratchy uniform for me!"

"The Mistress?" Mrs Axton questioned, "Came down here? I wonder what on earth has come over her? Well, good for you Anya. I suppose I'm too old to get new dresses, eh?"

"Don't be cross Mrs A..." I ventured but then saw the questioning look and speedily said, "Mrs Axton. I'm sure she'll get you one too.

"Oh, do be quiet, Anya. Now quick, Maud needs feeding and I've got plenty of work to be doing so that's your job."

"What shall I give her?" I asked setting my dress down delicately on my bed.

"Check the cupboards, I'm sure you'll soon figure something out. Make some carrot or cabbage soup which you can spoon-feed her with." With that, she left the room.

I rummaged through the kitchen cupboards and found some cabbage. It might not taste as good as carrot soup, but it would have to do. It turned out alright. Maud loved soup, so I prayed she had at least a bit more appetite to eat than the previous days and weeks. It had been three weeks almost and she didn't seem to be getting any better.

Mrs Axton had told me to cover my nose and mouth each time I went to see Maud. I couldn't find the old strip of fabric I had been using, so I ripped a strip of material from my old uniform and tied it around my lower face.

"Maud?" I called, though it sounded more like 'Mood' with the cloth over my mouth.

Maud was lying very still on her bed. Still as a statue. Her eyelids were shut tight and her mouth was twisted in the way it would be if you had sucked on a lemon sherbet. Her skin was pale — deathly pale, like all the colour had been sucked out of her.

"Maud?" I called again. Perhaps she was sleeping. Cautiously, I tiptoed over to her. It didn't even look like she was breathing.

I tried spooning some soup into her mouth, but her lips didn't even twitch, which was odd. I gave her a slight nudge even though I knew I had to touch her as little as possible. She didn't move.

With no other option, I put my head around Maud's door and shouted a few times for Mrs Axton."

"For heaven's sake, Anya," Mrs Axton cried bustling in, bucket in hand, "What is it no…"

She took one look at Maud, dropped the bucket and crashed down to Maud's side shaking her frantically. Nothing.

"Send for the doctor, Anya.

"Quick!" I knew all too well how to do that.

The only problem was I didn't know where the nearest doctor was.

"Anya?" Charles said bumping into me as I crashed downstairs

"We always seem to bump into each other. Where are you going?"

"No time, Charles. I'm sorry!" I stammered, apologising, "Its Maud. She has taken a turn for the worse. Much worse. I have to get to the hospital, and I have no clue where it is!"

"I'll take you," Charles offered, "I know old London like the back of my hand. Nelson Hospital is not too far off. Just at the edge of Wimbledon."

"Would you? Oh, thank you, Charles!" We ran through the busy streets.

"Up ahead!" Charles shouted.

Charles and I rushed into the hospital. It was unusually quiet. So different from the streets we'd just come from. By the time we got to Nelson Hospital, my hair was flapping limply and my chest was sticky with sweat.

Running up to the front desk I panted, "Please, Miss, my friend is very ill. She's been ill a while with scarlet fever. We need a doctor to come over to Tippets House and have a look at her urgently, please. She's hardly moving…"

"Say no more," the lady said,

"George, Harry and James, a scarlet fever case at Tippets House. Get going. Now!"

"Lead the way," George instructed, turning to me.

Charles and I jumped into the horse-drawn ambulance and we explained a little about Maud on our way to Tippets House. I willed the ambulance to move faster as it chugged along painfully slowly.

"This is it," I said breathlessly.

They bundled in carrying their medical cases.

"Where's the girl?" one of them asked.

"This way."

I led them up to Maud's room to find Mrs Axton stroking her hair and whispering something in her ear.

They checked her heart and listened to her breathing. Their expressions were grave, which was not a good sign. They shook their heads.

"Step outside please," one of them said to me and closed the door after me.

I pressed my ear against the door hoping to hear what was going on inside. Standing with me on the other side of the door, Charles hung his head, a melancholy look on his face.

"No…" I heard Mrs Axton sob. "No!"

I was frozen to the spot. It couldn't be. Surely not. Then the door opened. George stepped out.

"We're sorry," he said.

Then I ran. I ran to my room because I didn't want to go through it again. I flung myself on my bed as tears spilt down my cheeks. Not too long later, Mrs Axton came to my room.

"Anya dear girl, don't cry. We must chin up. It won't be long before the undertakers come for Maud and it will be your chance to say good-bye."

"What do you mean 'say good-bye?' Am I not going to her funeral?"

"I'm afraid it may not be possible Anya. We have to inform her family and they will arrange the funeral and decide who they want there. Master Edwards and the Mistress have been told and they are providing the help needed to take Maud to the funeral directors before her family comes down from Newcastle."

That broke my heart even more.

How desperately sad, that Maud would just be taken away like that with no opportunity to say bye-bye. I couldn't make myself move. It was all too much. First Mam, then having to experience this again with Maud. It was all too much.

Later that day, another carriage drew up outside. I had managed to go downstairs to tend to the front room. I needed to do something rather than lie there in my room, where all I could do was relive my ordeal over and over. First, it was Mam, then Maud. Death. Too much death. I peered through the curtains and saw some men run up the stairs with a stretcher. They rapped on the front door but I didn't move. I heard Mrs Axton come down the hall and open the front door.

"Follow me please," I heard her say.

I stood there transfixed to that spot. Before long, I saw them come back out with Mrs Axton and Charles descending the stairs behind them. Mrs Axton looked over to the left and saw me peering through the window. I could tell she had been crying. I watched in horror as they carted Maud into the back of the carriage and set off. Just like that. She was gone. Neither Mrs Axton nor Charles came to talk to me afterwards. I guess that each had to deal with the event in their own way. I couldn't remember if or how I finished cleaning the front room or how the rest of the day went. It was all a complete blur.

Everything from that day on went by so quickly. It felt as though life was a helter-skelter ride.

Continually having double the workload also ensured there was no time to sit and stare. Maud was dead. It was definite. Only Mrs Axton had been able to go to her funeral and burial. I found that unfair as I had spent a sufficient amount of time working at the house to allow me to attend. Some of Maud's family had come down from Newcastle; they were too poor to take her back home. Mrs Axton was entirely different after Maud's funeral. Instead of shouting and barking orders at me, she spoke in hushed tones, drifting absent-mindedly through the house sweeping and doing regular housework but without the same gusto she was previously renowned for.

For their part, the Master and Mistress became even more distant if that was possible. They had been horrified when they were informed, but I guess it was partly because of how guilty they felt to have a maid dying in their house without a doctor being called or being taken to hospital. Also, I wondered if they thought I too had scarlet fever and would infect Charity? It felt strange without Maud. I even missed her teasing and bickering. At least it gave some spirit to the servants' quarters.

Eventually, I'd managed to post my letter to Tad. Events surrounding Maud had taken over and I had lost the opportunity to post the letter that Friday. So, waiting for a reply from Tad or Mam-gu gave me something to look forward to. It helped me forget the drudgery of my days and lose myself in the feeling I would have when a received a reply. These days there was hardly any time to go out for a walk or explore the market to find young George to play with. Usually, after lunch, I could just about sneak off to my room during the day to catch a quick nap before it was time to get supper ready. There seemed to be no plans to find another maid to help out. It often made me wonder about the conversation I had heard Master Edwards have. Maybe there *were* money troubles at Tippets House.

* * *

About three weeks after Maud's passing, I heard Charles calling for me. Hurrying through the hall to the drawing-room, he held out his hand and handed me a letter.

"The postman has just been with a fresh set of letters and there's one for you," he said pointing to a stack of letters. I could just about make out my name imprinted on the one at the top. It was addressed in Tad's handwriting.

"It's for me!" I gasped rushing towards him. "That one's mine!"

"I know, I know," he said smiling. He picked it up and held it out to me.

I could have snatched his arm off, I was that eager.

"Thank you, Charles!" I shrieked dashing upstairs to my room with lightning speed.

Dear Anya,

Hello, darling. It's me, Tad. Thank you so much for your letter darling, it made me so happy.

Unfortunately, I am quite ill dear, but am thinking of you every second. I was in hospital but am now back home slowly recovering. Your mam-gu has kindly been around a few times to make me the occasional meal and tend to my needs. I get by somehow at other times. Old Mo and Pat (remember them?) have also been very kind. If I could just make it off this bed, I would tell you everything — about how terrible I feel for having ventured so far off course that I sent you to London. I am ever so sorry and do hope you can forgive me. I pray I will be better soon so I can make it up to you.

Anya, I love you. Never forget that. Whatever happens, do not forget that.

Love you always,
Tad.

It was a bittersweet experience reading Tad's letter. I was glad he was home from the hospital. That was some good news. I needed that for a change. He sounded a lot like the Tad I knew before everything became topsy-turvy. I missed him, Mam and home so badly that I ached. The pain of missing home was too much to bear; it gave me ample reason for a good cry. I shook myself and returned downstairs to continue with the rest of my day.

* * *

One sunny Sunday, when the sun was set high in the sky, a taxi stopped in front of the house. I was just about to finish with my work for the day, so I watched the woman inside faff about trying to open the door. It made me chuckle that that was how clueless I had been when I first arrived in London.

The woman who stepped out was old and frail but appeared regal, wearing a long velvet dress. She was sporting an unnecessarily big hat and her head was tilted so I couldn't see her face.

The woman rapped on the door.

"I'll get it," I called, quite intrigued to see who this strange woman was.

Opening the door, I greeted the woman with, "Hello, ma'am, what can I do for you?"

"Don't make me laugh, Anya," Mam-gu said looking up.

"Mam-gu?" I jumped into her arms with tears of joy, "Mam-gu! It's really you!"

"Course it's me!" Mam-gu exclaimed, "Oof! My 'ip!"

"Sorry, Mam-gu. What are you doing here? Is Tad alright?"

"Come to get you, you nana! And, your Tad is faring better than he has in a good long while," she replied.

"What about Mrs Axton and the Mistress and Master. Won't they be terribly cross?"

"I've sorted it all out with those fellows. Now come on, fetch Mrs Axton so I can see her in person. The train back to Cardiff leaves before sundown."

I dashed to the laundry room.

"Mrs Axton! My mam-gu's here! Did you know about this?

"Yes, indeed Anya. Your grandmother wrote to me some time ago stating her intentions of coming for you. A very persuasive woman I must say. You are a good hard-working girl Anya, but you are not cut out for this life."

207

I could have told you that for free from day one, I thought to myself.

"Now, go pack your belongings and say what good-byes you can while I talk to your grandmother."

"Why didn't you tell me, Mrs Axton?"

"Well, your grandmother asked for it to be that way, so you wouldn't stay too anxious for too long. Now go."

I flew upstairs, then threw my things as quickly as I could into my suitcase. Dashing quickly round the house, I said my good-byes to Charity, Charles and Mistress Edwards. Everyone seemed to know I was leaving but me.

When I got downstairs, Mam-gu had hailed another taxi and was at the foot of the stairs. Mrs Axton stood at the top of the stairs, smiling.

"Bye child. Take good care of yourself."

"Bye, Mrs Axton." I gave her a hug before leaping into the taxi and riding off. I put my head on Mam-gu's shoulder and for once in a very long time, it felt like I had a home and a family.

About the Author

Kirsten Mbawa is a twelve-year old, Year Seven student, one of the famed Mbawa Book Reviewers duo and winner of the 2015 Young Writers Talent for Writing Award. A voracious reader and book reviewer, Sagas of Anya is Kirsten's debut novel which honours her love for historical fiction. With this homage to one side, Kirsten plans to throw the boundaries of time and place to the wind by writing a piece of dystopian fiction for her next novel.

Kirsten lives in Northampton (where she was born) together with her parents, two sisters and pet cat

Zaki. In her spare time, Kirsten loves to dance, participate in gymnastics, and play tennis and the piano!

Connect with the Mbawa Book Reviewers by following the social media links below. Or search Mbawa Book Reviewers on YouTube — Don't forget to subscribe!

You can connect with me on:

⊕ http//mbawabooks.co.uk

▐ https//www.facebook.com/mbawabookreviewers

▣ https//www.instagram.com/mbawabookreviewers

🕊 https//twitter.com/mbawabookreview

Subscribe to my newsletter:

✉ http://mbawabooks.co.uk